OX

What's it like to be a rich kid? A guy who lives in a big house in Palm Beach, Florida, and gets taken to Mexico just to see a cow?

It's really not too much fun—especially if you're Franklin Olmstead and you're big and fat and cry a lot and all the kids call you Ox . . . and if you've got a father who doesn't care about that cow at all.

OX: THE STORY OF A KID AT THE TOP
by John Ney

BANTAM PATHFINDER EDITIONS

Bantam Pathfinder Editions provide the best in fiction and nonfiction in a wide variety of subject areas. They include novels by classic and contemporary writers; vivid, accurate histories and biographies; authoritative works in the sciences; collections of short stories, plays and poetry.

Bantam Pathfinder Editions are carefully selected and approved. They are durably bound, printed on specially selected high-quality paper, and presented in a new and handsome format.

OX: THE STORY
OF A KID AT THE TOP

BY JOHN NEY

BANTAM PATHFINDER EDITIONS
TORONTO / NEW YORK / LONDON

A NATIONAL GENERAL COMPANY

This low-priced Bantam Book
has been completely reset in a type face
designed for easy reading, and was printed
from new plates. It contains the complete
text of the original hard-cover edition.
NOT ONE WORD HAS BEEN OMITTED.

RLI: $\dfrac{\text{VLM (VLR 2-3)}}{\text{IL 5-up}}$

OX: THE STORY OF A KID AT THE TOP
*A Bantam Book / published by arrangement with
Little, Brown and Company*

PRINTING HISTORY
Little, Brown edition published March 1970
Bantam edition published September 1971
2nd printing

All rights reserved.
Copyright © 1970 by John Ney.
This book may not be reproduced in whole or in part, by
mimeograph or any other means, without permission.
For information address: Little, Brown and Company,
34 Beacon Street, Boston, Massachusetts 02106.

Published simultaneously in the United States and Canada

Bantam Books are published by Bantam Books, Inc., a National
General company. Its trade-mark, consisting of the words "Bantam
Books" and the portrayal of a bantam, is registered in the United
States Patent Office and in other countries. Marca Registrada.
Bantam Books, Inc., 666 Fifth Avenue, New York, N.Y. 10019.

PRINTED IN THE UNITED STATES OF AMERICA

For
JANET
the tiny
SCHEHERAZADE
who tells me those
wonderful Palm Beach tales

CHAPTER ONE

THE THING that gets me is — what future is there for a kid today? Like I live in Palm Beach and I'm supposed to have everything, but if I have everything how come I feel so lousy? All the time.

I'm supposed to be the kid at the top, and if *I* feel that lousy, how do the kids at the bottom feel? And the kids in the middle? You can hardly think about it.

And why do I have so many problems? Nothing is simple. It may start simple, but then it gets so you can't follow it. Like this composition about cows that I had to do last week.

It started on Tuesday. The sun was shining when I got up, but it shines almost every day in Palm Beach, so that doesn't mean anything. I watched television for an hour or so and then Rachel called me for breakfast. I ate some of it, but it wasn't very good. Mom and Dad were asleep, as usual. They sleep a lot.

Charles drives me to school every morning, and we went out to the garage together and Rachel came running after me with my lunch — she'd forgotten it until then, as usual. And it wasn't worth running for, anyhow.

Charles lit a cigar and started complaining

about Mom wanting him to drive her to Miami that day. "She wants to go to Miami," he said, "and your dad will have such a big hangover that he won't want to drive himself to the Everglades for that first drink, so he'll want me to drive him, too. Well, I can't be in two places at once. I told her last weekend — if you both want to be driven different places, you better get two chauffeurs."

"Aw, knock it off," I said. "Stop buggin' me."

"Buggin' *you!*" Charles said. "*I'm* the one who's getting bugged."

"I've got my own problems," I said. "I don't want yours, too."

"What problems does a twelve-year-old kid have?" he said, with that nasty sneer he has.

"What problems *doesn't* a twelve-year-old kid have?" I asked him straight, and that shut him up. Charles is so dumb that he forgets they're my parents and I know more about them than he does.

I got out at school without a word, and he didn't say anything, either. We separate that way every morning because we always have a fight about something.

The first kid I saw said, "Here comes the ox." I'm big for my age. And fat, too. I mean really big. I'm not as fat as I am big, but I'm fat enough. I guess it's puppy fat, because my grandfather —the one who made the money — was about six feet eight, and he was fat when he was young, too.

There are nine other kids in the fourth grade, and Mrs. Hollins is our teacher. I suppose she's the only person who understands me. I mean understands my problem and how it is at home. At first, I thought she was a sucker because she was nice to me, but then I figured out she was only nice to me because she was sorry for me and she wasn't weak at all. I should be in the sixth grade, so I'm two years behind, and I'm so big that I look like an elephant with the rest of the grade, but that doesn't bother her. "I may have you here in Fourth forever, Franklin," she says, "so it's fortunate we get on together."

She can take just one look at me in the morning and tell how bad it has been at home — like whether Dad's been sleeping on the lawn and Charles and I had to carry him in before I came to school, and all the rest. I can't let her know I know what she knows about me, though. It's all done like a secret joke.

Like that morning, she said, "Nice night, Franklin?"

"Swell," I said, and burst into tears. I cry a lot.

"Franklin's going to have a good cry," Mrs.

Hollins said, and I went out on the balcony. She told me that right at the beginning — that I should go out on the balcony when I wanted to cry. So I spend about half my time out there.

I told her one day that I was sorry I cried so much, and she told me not to give it another thought. "All the Greek heroes cried," she said. "Especially Achilles."

"That was the old days," I said.

"Well," she said, "in modern times, Winston Churchill was a great crier. It's a natural purge."

"What does 'purge' mean?" I asked her.

"Look it up," she said. That's a trick she has.

I did look it up in the class dictionary, about six weeks later, and could see what she meant. There was plenty I had to get rid of.

So I stood out on the balcony for a while and cried, and then the headmaster, Mr. Stokely, walked by down below and looked up and said, "Why aren't you in class, Franklin?"

I started to say I was crying, but then I changed it and said I was watering the plant exhibit.

"Very good," he said, and waddled away.

Then I went back into class and Mrs. Hollins knew from looking at me just what had happened with Mr. Stokley. I knew she knew.

The prettiest girl in the class is Natalie

Gregg. I guess she always thinks I'm some sort of barbarian because I'm such a mess and wear thongs and my hair is too long and I can't play football. But Mrs. Hollins always says, "All the girls love you, Franklin, because you're so helpless." I wonder whether she means Natalie, too. I think she does, but I don't know if she's right. She's right about everything else, though, so I suppose she's right about Natalie.

But it's hard to believe when you think how Natalie looks at me. Her family is Gregg Shipping Lines, New York, and they've had money for a long time, so she has background. Which is what I don't have, and I mean *don't have*, even if I am rich. There aren't many kids in Palm Beach with background, so when somebody does have it, like Natalie Gregg, you can't miss them.

But what I wonder is — what good is it going to do her? She'll probably have to marry some slob like me in the end and all that background will just be wasted.

Our fourth grade is so lousy, when you come right down to it, that there's no one else in it who's as interesting as I am, mess or not. Of course, there are only three other boys in it, but you'd think one of them would be better than I am. But they aren't.

Like Tommy Alterdale. When I cry, he yells

"Rowboat!" and pretends he's rowing in an ocean of tears that I'm supposed to be filling up the room with. Very funny, but no one thinks so except him.

He's about the only kid I ever met who has less background than I do. His money comes from Alterdale Container Corporation, somewhere in Wisconsin.

It's so boring in class that I go to the bathroom a lot. "Come on, Franklin," Mrs. Hollins says when I start getting nervous, "we want fifteen uninterrupted minutes of your company."

"I have to go to the bathroom," I say. "I'm only a kid."

"Well, go ahead," she says. "It's better than having you wiggling and twitching in here."

So I spend about half my time in the bathroom.

No, I'm only kidding. I'm in class a lot, when you come right down to it.

We have a sensitive plant in the class that closes its leaves when you touch it, and I touch it a lot. It opens up when you stop touching it, so you can touch it again and make it close. I walk over and touch it when I get bored with everything else, and Mrs. Hollins says, "Franklin, stop touching that plant!"

"I'm having a science lesson," I say, and sometimes everyone laughs. But I've said it so often that not many of the kids laugh anymore.

I was touching the sensitive plant last Tuesday and Mrs. Hollins said, "Franklin seems so fond of science, perhaps he'll tell us how butter is made from milk."

"That's not science," I said. "Science is atoms and blast-offs and going to the moon. Vaaarrr-ooooooooom!"

But she kept nagging at me and I had to tell her that I didn't know anything about milk or butter or eggs or any of the rest of that stuff except that you eat it.

Then she asked the rest of the class and no one knew much more than I do.

"Haven't any of you ever been to a farm she asked us.

We all said "Sure," but it turned out we meant farms where they have racehorses, like the one Jerry Carter's father has in Ocala. No one knew much about that other kind.

"Such deprived children," Mrs. Hollins said. "You remind me of a class I had a few years ago in the slums in New York City. None of those children had ever seen a cow either."

"I've seen cows!" I said. "Gosh, Mrs. Hollins, what do you take me for? Some kind of poor kid? It's just that I don't know how they work!"

"It's time you learned," she said. "One week from today, I want a composition from everyone in this class on cows. How they 'work,' as Franklin says, and what they produce — everything about them. At least three or four pages."

I howled about that because I can't write compositions. My spelling is really lousy and I can't express myself. But I'm not too serious when I howl because I don't do much homework anyhow.

This time it was different — at least it was different in a way — because when I got home Dad was sitting around with nothing to do, all shaved and cleaned up and having a drink by the pool.

He made me sit down and talk to him, and started giving me a long speech about how I might have to work when I grew up because taxes would take all the money, so I better get ready to go to college. And to go to college, I had to get better grades in school and get out of the fourth grade. He always gives me a speech when he's had a big night and is getting ready for a bigger one.

"The time to start is now," he said. "Do you have any homework?"

And that was where I made my big mistake, because I said, "Yeah, I'm supposed to do a composition on cows for next week."

"Cows!" he said, looking like he needed another drink in a hurry.

"Cows," I said. "Mrs. Hollins found out that none of us kids in Palm Beach know anything about cows, so we have to do a composition on how they make milk and butter and the rest of that stuff."

"Bill Waverly has a ranch over near Fort Myers," he said, like he was the father interested in the kid's problem in a usual family. "I could run you up there."

Wasn't it typical? Any other family would have looked up "Cows" in a book, in one of those sets where they have all those things listed. Even most rich families have them. But, of course, we didn't have *any* books except the TV schedule and my comic books, so the best he could come up with was a trip to Fort Myers!

"Come on," he said, "let's go."

I thought he was kidding, but he was standing up and ready to go.

"It takes three hours to drive over there," I said, "and we won't be there until seven and then we won't be back until ten . . ."

"We'll rent a helicopter at the airport," he said. "We'll be there and back in a couple of hours."

Boy, do you not want to see Mom tonight, I was thinking.

So we went out and rented the helicopter, and the pilot took us over to the west coast. It's about a hundred miles. Halfway there I remembered I didn't have any paper or anything to take notes, so I'd have to depend on my memory, which was not too good anyhow. At the end of the day it was worse.

CHAPTER TWO

DAD HAD CALLED Mr. Waverly and he was waiting outside at his ranch when the helicopter landed and so were a lot of his friends. The blades made the wind blow and they were all yelling because the ladies' skirts were waving around, but I don't know what all the fuss was about because they were already so short they didn't wave much.

Dad made a lot of noise about how I had never seen a cow and how I had to write a composition and everyone thought that was so cute. And a couple of the ladies messed up my hair and said I was good-looking even if I was fat. I didn't like them fooling with my hair, even if it always is messy anyhow, but what can you do about it? They always go for your hair and give it a couple of swipes and tell you how good-looking you are even if you are fat, and then walk off and never know you again.

"But we don't have *cows* here," Mr. Waverly yelled at Dad. "This is a *beef* ranch!"

And everyone laughed at that, especially Dad, and then they all went out to the patio for more drinks.

"Listen, son," Mr. Waverly said before he walked off, "you go out to the barns and get one

of the men to show you around. You might learn
something about cattle, anyhow."

So I went out to the barns and there was a
thin little man there with one of those Southern
accents, and he had blue jeans on, and he took
me around. His name was Ed. He was a worker,
but he knew all about the "spread," as he called
it. There were a lot of those all-black cattle in
special stalls, and they had big silver chains
around their necks. They looked happy, but
they weren't cows. I didn't dare tell the man
who was taking me around that I was supposed
to find out about cows, because I knew he was a
worker and it just would have sounded crazy to
him that a kid my age was flying around in a
helicopter to look at cows.

I thanked him for all his help, and went back
to the house to get Dad, but he didn't want to go
because they were all having such a good time.
So I ate dinner in the kitchen. It was pretty
good, some kind of pigeon pie. The servants
gave it to me. After dinner I took a nap on a
sofa and when I woke up about eleven the party
was still going on and there was a lot of noise.
Th helicopter was still parked out in the field
and the pilot was at the party, too. It looked as
though we were going to be there all night, so
I went back to my sofa and rolled up for the

night. At least I wouldn't have to go to school
the next day.

It was quiet in the morning, and I knew no
one would be up until around noon, so I had
about four or five hours to kill. I looked for a
television set and found a color one in a little
room like a den, and settled down. Same old
stuff, but what else was there to do?

One of the servants gave me breakfast and
asked me how I slept and I said it was lousy.

"You should have found yourself a real bed,"
she said.

"Someone else might have come along later,"
I said. "It's safer to pick out a sofa. I know that
from experience."

She was a pretty good cook. Sausage and eggs
and a few pancakes. I knew it would make me
fatter, but I didn't have much to do except eat.

"I was just finishing when Ed, the little
worker who took me through the barns the
night before, came running in, all excited.

"The Indians!" he squealed. "Down near the
pump on section thirty-eight. They've got 'em!"

He was so excited he got me excited and I
started yelling "What? Where?" like some kind
of nut.

"No time to tell you now," he said. "Come
on!"

We ran outside and jumped in a pickup and

he jammed it in gear and we tore off down a dirt
road with a cloud of dust like an atom mush-
room behind us.

"They're rustlers!" Ed said. "They're stealing
cattle!"

"Who is?" I yelled. The pickup was so noisy
you couldn't hear a thing.

"The Indians," he said. "The Indians from
the reservation. Jack Ellery and Tom caught
'em redhanded."

His little face was screwed up and you could
tell it was going to be hard on those Indians.
Up behind us was a rifle in a rack.

We got to where they had them in about
twenty minutes. It was way out in the middle of
nowhere. There were two fences that crossed
and then went off as far as you could see in
straight lines, and a big irrigation ditch and a
pump. It was what they called reclaimed glade-
land. They build irrigation ditches and clean it
all up and get grass growing. About a mile
from where we were you could see the real
glades begin though, low and flat and covered
with that bushy grass that's out there.

There were three Indians and two white
workers and four cattle standing there. They all
looked as though they didn't know what they
were doing. One of the workers had a rifle. The
Indians were Seminoles, you could tell because

they had shirts on with that Seminole design. Anyhow, like Mrs. Hollins says, Seminoles are the only kind of Indians there are in Florida. They looked tired and dirty, just like the ones you see in the tourist places on the way to Miami. One of them was big, like the kind that wrestle alligators in those places, and the other two were little and skinny.

"We got 'em cold, Ed," one of the workers said. "They was tryin' to take them steers through the fence yonder."

He pointed at the fence and sure enough, there was a place where the wire was cut and bent back to make a big hole. I was looking at the hole and at the Indians, too, but I was thinking about the man saying "yonder." It was the kind of word you read in those old books, and you never think you're going to hear it in real life. But in the backwoods of Florida you can hear anything — that's what Dad always says and it's true. "They all came from Georgia originally," he says, "and they've been marinating out in those glades for a hundred years so they're really pretty ripe Crackers."

Ed walked over and took a look at the fence, and then walked back. He walked slowly, and when he got back he just stood there looking at the Indians. He had taken the rifle out of the pickup and was holding it like a snake. The

Indians shifted a little and looked right back at him. The sun was already hot and the workers were sweating, but the Indians weren't. I was soaking wet myself, of course. I wanted to tell Ed to take me back, but I could tell he was so excited in that quiet mean way that he wasn't going to leave until he'd done what he wanted. He looked dangerous, so I kept my mouth shut.

"You know what the law says about rustlin'?" he shot out at the Indians.

They didn't say anything.

Ed moved the rifle muzzle up until it was pointing dead at the big one's heart.

"I asked you a question," he said, low and mean. "You know what the law says about rustlin'?"

They still didn't say anything.

"You better give me an answer," he said.

They didn't say anything, and then he cocked the rifle. The click sounded terrible out there in the heat. The Indians didn't look afraid or anything, though, and I could tell they were just going to take what was coming without a word. They'd been caught and they were going to take anything that happened. I guess that's the way they are. If something is going to happen anyhow, they don't see any sense in fighting it. And making a fool out of yourself arguing and whining.

You had to admire them for that. Especially when you're like me and don't have any guts at all. If I'd been standing there where they were I'd have been crying and rolling around and begging for my life. Even as it was, I was the first one to crack. We were all standing there in the sun and that click when Ed cocked the rifle was the last thing we'd heard and the seconds were dragging out and no one was moving. It was just straight tension, and so hot you felt like fainting. I couldn't stand it.

"You can't do anything to them," I said to Ed. My voice sounded like an old record, all shaky and wobbly, but he turned around and looked at me.

"Stay out of this kid," he said. "You don't know nothin' about it."

"Yes, I do," I said. I was trying to imitate the way Dad and his friends talk to workers. Sort of loud and swaggering, with all your teeth showing. "My dad told me all about it. The law can't do anything to anyone about rustling if the cattle *are still on your side of the fence*."

It was the first thing that came into my head and I was praying they *were* on the right side of the fence. But I thought I was safe because there was grass on both sides of the fence and if there was grass it was still the ranch. This wasn't the outside fence.

"You don't know nothin' about it," Ed said, but I could tell by his voice that he wasn't all that sure.

"You have to find them outside," I said. "That's what all the law experts say."

"He might be right, Ed," one of the other workers said. "Let's just take 'em in."

"And get sued?" I said. I felt like I was really warming up. "You take them in and they've got a lawsuit against you for . . . for the wrong kind of arrest. Because the cattle are still on the inside of the fence. Do you want to cost Mr. Waverly about nine million dollars?"

"They cut the fence," Ed said. "That's destroying property and trespass, and don't tell me it ain't."

He had me stopped there, and I couldn't think of anything to say until I looked at the Indians again, and remembered they wouldn't say anything no matter what I said.

"You can cut fence out in the glades if you're dying of thirst or something," I said.

"Them Indians ain't dyin' of no thirst," Ed said. I wish Mrs. Hollins could have heard the way he talked. She thinks we're bad on grammar, but she should hear someone like Ed.

"All right," I said. "So they're not. But let me give you a tip. Mr. Waverly's giving a party at the house. If you show up with a bunch of dirty Indians and bother him, he'll be sore at you. Even if you take them to jail yourself, the police will call him back about it. They always do. I know. And then he'll be sore at you because you interrupted his fun. He'll say, 'Those Indians didn't get anything, did they? You could have just patched the fence, couldn't you? Why are you bothering me?' It would be different if there was nothing else going on. But you interrupt a party and you're in trouble. Don't say I didn't tell you."

It was my last try. Ed stood there, thinking it over and waving the rifle around and I thought he was going to do something after all, but then he finally let down the hammer carefully with his thumb and lowered the muzzle.

"If I ever catch you on this place again," he said to the Indians, "I'll shoot first and talk afterwards. Now, get."

The Indians didn't say anything or show anything. They just turned around and walked right through that hole in the fence.

I was so weak I could hardly make it over to the pickup. Ed told the other men to fix the fence and then he climbed into the pickup, too, and we started back. He didn't say a word all the way and neither did I.

But I was ready for him when we stopped.

"I'm not saying anything about this to Mr.

Waverly or anyone else," I said. "Not even my dad."

"Now isn't that nice of you," he said, with a mean curl to his lip.

"You're sore at me because you wanted to blast those Indians," I said. "But you ought to thank me for talking you out of it."

"Thanks," he said, still mean.

"And I was right about not bothering Mr. Waverly, too," I said. "I bet when you think about what happened you *will* thank me."

"I said 'thanks,'" he said, but I couldn't tell whether he meant it or not. Probably not. You can never do much with those little workers who have that mean streak. One like Ed would rather put a bullet in an Indian than do anything else. Even eat.

I got out of the pickup and went back in the house and sat around for a while. There was nothing very good on television.

The helicopter pilot was the first one up and he didn't look so good. Then everyone else started drifting in, and there was all the squealing for an "eye-opener" and they were off again. The helicopter pilot wanted to stay, I could tell, but they got rid of him. They always keep people like that around for a night, but they get tired of them during the day.

One of the ladies tried to get me to drink some

of her bullshot, but I told her I never touch the
stuff and that she'd be sorry if she did herself
on an empty stomach. She laughed and said she
knew what she could do and what she couldn't
do.

Her name was Clive, but it didn't sound like a
girl's name to me. She was young and pretty
good-looking and she started playing up to me
to make an impression on Dad, asking me all
about what I did, and I told her a lot of stuff.

I told her about some poor kids I know. They
live in Palm Beach, but the father is a dentist
and works. One of the kids is my age and goes
to the public school, but I met him on the Trail
one day and he asked me to his house. I wasn't
doing anything so I went. I had no idea people
lived like that in Palm Beach. It was so small
and cramped and everything ran over on to
everything else. Then the father came home and
he wanted to do a crossword puzzle and the only
table he could get to had watermelon seeds all
over it and he had to push them off and then put
the paper down on the wet table. He'd been filling teeth all day or something and he looked at
me like an old dog that's lost its bone.

"But a man like that isn't poor," Clive said.
"A dentist who can live in Palm Beach isn't
poor."

"Sure, he's poor," I said. I didn't understand what she meant.

"Well, you have a funny idea of poverty," she said.

"I know it's a poor house," I said. "If I didn't know any other way, there were all those Barbie dolls all over the place."

"You have to have money to buy those," Clive said.

"But only poor people buy them," I said. I saw what she didn't understand now. "A lot of poor people get money once in a while, and then they buy stuff for their kids instead of for themselves. I never saw a rich kid with Barbie dolls. Because rich kids can't push their parents around the way poor kids can. Did you read what Art Buchwald said about those Barbie dolls? About all those poor people laying out about three thousand dollars for Barbie dolls just because their kids wanted them?"

"No," she said.

"You ought to," I said. "He can really make you see it."

"So you think it's better to be rich?" she asked me, kind of changing the subject.

"Are you kidding?" I said.

"So do I," she said, and then her face started to turn green in front of me, just like I knew it was going to, and she got up in a hurry and tore off to be sick. I can always tell when they're going to do that. Most of them drink so much that they can take a few before brunch with no effects, but I can spot the ones who can't.

"Well, Franklin," Dad said to me, "did you find out all about cows?"

"Aw, Dad," I said. "Mr. Waverly told you last night that this is a beef ranch. There aren't any milk cows here at all."

"What about Lucille?" some other guy horned in, laughing and snorting around. "What about my wife? You want to look at a cow, kid, I'll show you a cow. I'll . . ."

"Lay off, George," Dad said. "This kid's got homework to do."

Dad can do that better than anyone I know. Get right in the spirit of a big party and then get moral all of a sudden and pull the rug out. The guy who'd been talking to him wasn't really like Dad and Mr. Waverly. He was only pretending to have money and loaf. You can always tell, and Dad can really pull the rug on them.

"Listen, Franklin," Dad said, "I brought you over here to see a cow, and I'm going to find a cow if it takes all day. If I have to *buy* one."

"Aw, gee, Dad, you don't have to do that," I said. I hate it when he gets like that. All serious and his eyes stick out, and he talks too slow.

"I never go back on a promise," he said, and

everyone was listening, and that made it worse. "I never go back on a promise, especially to a kid. Especially to my own kid. Isn't that right, Franklin?"

"I don't know," I said. "Oh, sure, that's right, Dad. You always keep your promises."

"That's right," Dad said. "And don't you forget it."

He sort of gets the problem off his mind that way, and then he can forget it.

The whole bunch of them partied around there until about four o'clock and then they had a few swims and took naps and about six they were all rested and cleaned up and ready for the cocktail hour. I'd been watching television all afternoon, and I was pooped, but they were fresh and ready to talk about cows again. They'd kind of forgotten about them during the day, but now it was funny again, and I could tell they were going to make something big out of it.

"They have cows in California," Mr. Waverly said. "I know, because I've seen them out there."

"So have I," Dad said. "Somewhere around Burlingame."

"Does Harry Ming still live out there?" Mr. Waverly said.

"I think he does," Dad said. "I haven't seen Harry for a long time."

"Seems a shame to let so much time go by without seeing Harry," Mr. Waverly said.

"Sure does," Dad said.

"Well?" Mr. Waverly said.

"There's the telephone," Dad said.

They thought it up, but everyone else there was all for it, too. It was such a good story to tell their friends. "We went to California to show Barry Olmstead's kid a cow."

CHAPTER THREE

IT'S ONLY about a five-hour flight to California, but by the time we got over to Miami and got out of there, we were up the whole night. There was a change in Chicago or someplace, and the whole bunch piled on and off. I slept most of the way, and had a pretty good dinner and some kind of breakfast. I had steak for dinner, and melon and eggs for breakfast. I had a lousy taste in my mouth, though, and my back was stiff from sleeping in the seat. Clive tried to rub my back, but it didn't help.

People talk a lot about California, and I guess it's all right. But it's always so hard to get there and once you've seen part of it, the rest is the same. This Harry Ming was supposed to meet us in San Francisco, but he didn't make it, so they rented a few limousines and we started for Pebble Beach, which is about two hundred miles away. But first they wanted to stop in San Francisco to tank up, so we went to the St. Francis Hotel and they made a lot of noise in the bar.

Then we got in the cars again and started to drive, but they wanted to stop about every ten minutes and the day really dragged along.

And every time we saw a cow, they'd all yell,

"Look at the cow, Franklin," and I was supposed to think that was funny.

And then Clive got sick, and Dad blew up at her.

I was thinking about what Mrs. Hollins would have made of it, and whether any of the kids she had in the slums in New York City ever had to travel around so much to find out about cows for a composition. Probably not. It was just too expensive. I wondered whether I should call her and tell her I was working on it. But she would have told me I was just missing school on purpose, and so I decided not to.

Well, the Ming place wasn't too bad when we finally got there. At first, it looked like any other house. Just big, and facing the ocean. Maybe more shrubbery than we get in Palm Beach, and more curves on the pool, but pretty much the same otherwise, and I was ready for the usual boring time. But then Vinnie Ming came along, a kid my own age who sees things about the same way.

He took me off to see the television in his bedroom, and when we got in there he didn't try to make a big deal out of anything, or talk or anything like that. We just sat and watched and the maid brought our dinners up and we ate them there. I asked him if he didn't have to go down and eat in the kitchen.

"Naw," he said. "Dad says the farther away the better, and that suits me, too."

I was pretty impressed because I'd never known a kid who got to eat like that, away from everyone. The maid was Chinese or something. Quiet, not like Rachel. She set the table up for us without arguing and we could eat and go right on watching television. There wasn't any distraction. You couldn't even hear the party. I've never been in a place like that before, and I had to admit that Vinnie Ming has one of the best deals of any kid I know. Even the dinner was good. Steak and a big baked potato and nothing else.

We knocked off about ten o'clock and I had the room next to his, with a real bed in it, so I got the first night's sleep since we left.

He had the television going the next morning when I woke up, and the Chinese maid brought breakfast in and set it up again. The breakfast was kind of strange, with club sandwiches instead of eggs or anything, but Vinnie said that he got tired of waiting until lunch to eat his club sandwich, so he always had it for breakfast. You kind of enjoy it, at that.

I told him some confidential stories when we were watching television. Like about Dale Tifton, in Palm Beach, who's a really tough kid because he's been practically brought up on the streets. I met him one day and he was going down to Worth Avenue to buy his own birthday present. And that night he had to sleep in the jail because his mom had gone over to the Bahamas and there was no one else at home, and he said, "I don't want the house to burn down when I'm asleep, so I always go to jail for the night when Mom's not around." The cops said they always had a room for him. I saw him coming out of the jail one morning when I was going to school, but I didn't wave or anything because I didn't see any reason to let the cops know we knew each other. I might be there myself someday.

Vinnie said that Dale sounds like a kid you can count on, and I said he was, but that he was too tough because he'd been on the streets too much.

Dale is so tough they can't let him in a school. He used to be in schools — he was even in our school for about a week, until he pushed Mr. Glover off the second-floor balcony — now he doesn't go to school at all. His father is Carl Tifton, the one whose brother runs American Cynadine. Carl Tifton is like Dad, he doesn't do anything. But he's gone all the way with it. He doesn't hunt or play tennis or anything *except* drink, and he weighs about four hundred pounds and sleeps all day every day and is only

up at night. He has a house in the north end of
Palm Beach and one in the south end. Dale says
it's because he never wants to be too far from
home. He won't have a thing to do with Dale
since he and Dale's mother were divorced. She's
been remarried about sixteen times. "I've had
more dads than all you other kids in Palm Beach
put together," Dale says and I can see what he
means even though it probably isn't *that* many.
She lives in a little apartment on Chilean. Dale
is supposed to have a bedroom there, but usually
some guest has it, so he's practically pushed out
and that's why they say he's always on the
streets. When the old-time Palm Beach ladies
drive by in their Rolls-Royces in the afternoon
they wrinkle their noses when they see him and
jabber to each other about him. Dale says what
they're saying is: "Look at that! Carl Tifton's
boy, a tramp! I hear he sleeps in the street, and
his father must have two hundred million dollars if he has a cent. Thank heavens Holly didn't
live to see him!"

Dale's probably right about what they say,
because everyone talks about the Tifton money.
Even my parents. It isn't that it's so much, for
Palm Beach anyhow — it's the difference between how much there is and the way Dale lives.
Even the way his father lives. He has the two
houses, but all the furniture is busted up in both

of them and he won't let anyone in to clean or
anything. I've never been in them, but Dale told
me. You can tell there's something funny just
looking at them from the outside, though. The
grass is about six feet tall and everything is
falling down, even the trees, because they never
get cleaned up after a hurricane or anything.
And there are rotten coconuts everywhere.
What makes it even harder for people to understand is that once the Tiftons were *it* in Palm
Beach. Dale's great-grandmother, Holly Tifton,
was the most important hostess here years and
years ago, and had the biggest house ever built
in Palm Beach. It was called Kail and had about
a thousand rooms. Dale's father was born there,
but it was torn down before Dale was born.
It used to take up about half the north end of
Palm Beach and you can still see pictures of it.
So people think of all that, too, when they look
at Dale. And I suppose that's the real reason
they don't try to make him go to school at all.

I told Vinnie all that and he was pretty interested.

Then I told him about our fourth grade and
how lousy it was, and how I was in a pretty
good fourth grade a couple of years ago, but the
rest of them since had been so boring. Not Mrs.
Hollins, but the other kids. Then he told me

about the fifth grade he's in. He's only behind one year.

Then he said, "What's all the talk about these cows?

And I told him about Dad making me come with him, and he told me about a trip *his* father took to Honolulu last year to pick some flowers from the top of a volcano for his mother or something.

"He took off without a suitcase or anything," Vinnie said, "and came back with about sixteen new bags, all matched, and said he hadn't been to Honolulu after all. He'd gone the other way, to Trinidad, and forgot all about the flowers."

Then one of Vinnie's sisters came in and we all watched television for a while. Her name is Jennifer and she's not as pretty as Natalie Gregg.

She told me the Ming money comes from some substitute for linoleum.

Then I had to tell her about my grandfather Olmstead inventing the way tires were made in the old days, and how he had a lot of other patents and was a genius, and how we got our money.

It was not bad listening to myself going along, but sort of boring, too. But that's what happens when you get a girl around. Vinnie and I were having a good time, and then Jennifer came along and it changed. She wanted to know who *I* was, so she told me who *she* was. They all work that way. My own sisters, Terry and Beth, do the same thing.

Dad came in before lunch and said, "I don't know why you kids always hang around that television. Why don't you get outside? We're going to play some golf. Franklin, you take a walk or go sailing or do something."

"O.K.," I said. He'd forgotten about the cows. Or didn't want to remember them. He didn't look too bad, and I guess he must have had a pretty good sleep.

I asked him if he thought we ought to call Mom, and he just said, "No."

I didn't want to call her much myself. It only would have meant an argument. It was Friday, so she probably knew we were gone for the weekend.

So Vinnie and I went out to take a walk after lunch, and he showed me the ocean and the cypress trees they have there and we threw a few rocks at a seal but didn't hit it.

We started back to the house, but then we remembered we weren't supposed to get back there too soon, so Vinnie said we should go see Mrs. Appleton, who lives on the same road he does.

"She's an old lady," he said, "but she's not the way most of them are."

I asked him what he meant by that, and he said, "You know how most of them are — they never really look at you when they talk to you."

"Yes," I said. I was thinking of the old people I know, and he was right. "They all act like they're going to be shot or something," I told him.

"That's what they look like, all right," Vinnie said.

"My own grandmother acts that way," I said. "She used to be kind of pulled together, but then after my grandfather died she started wearing stretch pants and dyed her hair orange and drives a convertible."

"Do you have just one grandmother?" Vinnie asked me.

"I always think of it that way," I told him. "I guess my mother has parents, but no one ever says anything about them because they never had any money. I asked my mom about them and she brushed me off. I asked her where she came from, and she said from an old Southern family. But Dad met her in New York or someplace when she was a model, and if there is an old Southern family down there somewhere, no one wants to think about them. That must mean they have no money."

"Couldn't mean anything else," Vinnie said, agreeing with me. "Probably farmers or what they call sharecroppers."

I didn't know what a sharecropper was, so he explained it, and I thought that sounded about right.

"There are people down there who don't even get enough to eat," Vinnie said. "You see programs about it on TV all the time."

"I hope they're not depending on my mom," I said.

"I guess my family is a little more careful than yours," Vinnie said. "I mean, neither one of my grandmothers would wear stretch pants or dye their hair like that. I suppose it's because we worry about what the old families in San Francisco think about us."

"Nobody worries about stuff like that in Palm Beach," I told him. "They just drink and yell at each other."

"That sounds better," Vinnie said. "More out in the open."

"I'm not so sure," I said. "Maybe it's better the other way."

We talked like that for about five minutes, each one of us saying the other way was better, and then I said, "I don't think it makes all that much difference — no matter how you look at it, a kid has a hard time today."

Vinnie said that was what he believed, too, and then we were walking up Mrs. Appleton's driveway and we didn't say anything more.

The butler opened the door and I could see right away that he was a real butler and not the kind they have in most houses. For nine out of ten butlers, they go to one of those agencies and hire them, or they go to England or Switzerland, and the butler always tells you where he used to work and complains about everything and stays about two years. But there's another kind that's been with families for years and years, and that's the kind Mrs. Appleton had. His name was Lansing, and he said to Vinnie, "Mrs. Appleton is in the garden. I'm sure she'd like to see you, but just to be positive, why don't you wait here for a moment and I'll tell her."

So we sat down on two chairs and waited. We didn't say anything to each other, but it wasn't that we wanted to talk and didn't. It was different than that, it was because it was so kind of quiet and peaceful in that house that you enjoyed being quiet. There was a calm that drifted right into you.

Then Lansing came back and we followed him through the house and out to the garden. All the rooms were quiet and had the same sort of calm. It's a hard thing to explain, because when there's nothing going on at our house you'd think it would be just as quiet but it isn't. There are still echoes or something coming off the walls and out of the furniture. Vinnie's house is not so much like that, but still enough so you can feel it. I looked at Vinnie and I could tell that he was wondering if I was noticing the quiet, so I nodded my head to show him I was.

Mrs. Appleton was sitting in a big wicker chair and she shook hands with Vinnie and he introduced me. Then I shook hands, too, and we sat down.

"I was about to have tea," Mrs. Appleton said, "and you should really join me. Will you?"

We said we would, and she asked Lansing to bring the tea.

She didn't ask me questions, the way most people do. She just went ahead with her sewing, and talked with Vinnie about his dog, and then he told her I was from Palm Beach.

"Palm Beach!" Mrs. Appleton said. "I was there years ago. The Royal Poinciana was still standing. And the Coconut Grove."

"I've heard people talk about them," I said. "But it's a lot different now."

"I can imagine," she said.

There was a sort of silence, and then I told her I lived there with my parents, and that my grandmother lived there, too.

"How nice," Mrs. Appleton said.

"Yes," I said.

And then Vinnie laughed and said we'd been talking about which was better, Palm Beach or Pebble Beach, and we started telling her about each one. Only instead of being honest about what we really thought, we talked as though we believed it. Like I said, "Palm Beach is better because it's not formal." And I told her about my grandmother being so informal. And Vinnie said, "I like Pebble Beach because the people think more about what other people think of them." And he told her about how *his* grandmother got into some club in San Francisco.

"I suppose there is a great deal to be said for both places," Mrs. Appleton said, "although I must say that Palm Beach sounds more open, as you put it. It must be refreshing to see women like your grandmother leading such an active life."

She didn't smile or anything when she said that, but I didn't think she could be serious about meaning it. She was a little like Mrs. Hollins that way, because Mrs. Hollins can say things she doesn't mean to kind of wake you up.

Then Lansing brought the tea, and it was something.

"I hope you like it," Mrs. Appleton said.

"I will," I said, and I did. There were the kinds of rolls and buns and biscuits that you never see except in a bakery. And special jams. "This is a real change for me," I told Mrs. Appleton. "You know how kids today eat."

"No, I don't," she said. "How do they eat?"

"Well, sandwiches and stuff like that between meals," I said. "You don't see food like this much. But I think it's better."

"It's the way kids used to eat," Vinnie said. "The whole life used to be different. Mrs. Appleton knows all about it."

"Oh, but of course," Mrs. Appleton said. "When I was your age, the automobile was a novelty. Naturally, things have changed since then."

"But wasn't it better for kids then?" I asked her.

"I could say yes," she said, "but I'm not so sure that was really the case. It's very difficult to remember another time accurately, to know whether you're being fair when you're my age and trying to remember what it was like in the distant past. To be perfectly honest, every age has its good points and bad points."

We talked some more like that, and then she told us about when she was a little girl. Her mother had married an Englishman who was in the army. He was a tall man with a beard, and they had seven children, and Mrs. Appleton could remember lunch on Sunday in their house in the country when they all sat down to what they called a "joint of beef." It was more like dinner than lunch and none of the children were allowed to talk.

"We girls were in our starched frocks, and the boys were in their jackets, and there wasn't a sound except for the quiet conversation between my mother and father. It was the only meal of the week we took with them, and it was considered such a treat to be allowed to eat with adults that we wouldn't have dreamed of behaving other than perfectly. One of us asked the blessing at the start of each meal, and another gave thanks at the end, and then we all stood up when my father did and he smiled at us and walked from the room like a general on parade and we walked behind him. It was very formal, but we didn't know anything else, so we thought it was the most wonderful life possible. . . .

"That was before the Great War, the 1914–1918 war, in which my father was killed. But after that war, nothing was quite the same again. My mother moved back to the United States, to San Francisco, and we were all brought up as Americans. But even when we went back to England to see friends in the same kind of house we had had and with the same kind of father— there were a few of them who hadn't been killed — it wasn't the same as it had been. The world was too different outside, so the men with the beards who carved joints while the children sat silently just seemed old-fashioned. That's the law of life, that everything changes, and now when I think of my girlhood I don't know whether it was as serene and lovely as I remember it or whether it was always slightly old-fashioned."

She told us a little more about those old days, and then she looked like she was getting tired, so Vinnie and I said we had to go.

"It was very nice of you to come," she said to both of us. She didn't say "very nice of you boys to come"—she just said "very nice of *you* to come."

Then we shook hands with her and she looked each one of us straight in the eye. She didn't say anything when she looked you in the eye and didn't give you any advice. She just looked straight at you like there was no advice to give. You'd have to do it for yourself.

After we left, we were walking back along the road and Vinnie said, "What do you think?"

"About what?"

"Well, Mrs. Appleton says you can't tell whether things used to be better or not. You only know they were different. Do you think that's right?"

"I don't know. How can a kid know a thing like that?"

"Just because you're a kid is no reason you shouldn't have an idea."

"All right, what's your idea?" I asked him. I could tell he was working around to telling me what he thought.

"I think Mrs. Appleton is sorry for us," he said. "I think she knows things used to be better. But she doesn't want to say so because she thinks it would hurt our feelings."

Vinnie stopped walking when he said that, and looked at me like he was asking a question. I could see what he meant about Mrs. Appleton. Listening to her was like seeing what used to happen as though you were there. When she talked about her father with the beard and the room where they had dinner, you could see it better than when they have a show on TV and take you back in time in a machine. There was the feeling of it.

Of course it was better then. I mean, things are so rotten for a kid now that anything would be better, no matter how long ago it was. You didn't need to talk to a nice old lady to know that, and I was wondering why Vinnie was acting like you had to talk to people to find it out.

I was opening my mouth to tell him that, and then I thought to myself. If he doesn't know it, maybe he keeps it from himself because he can't stand it. Maybe he isn't strong enough to stand it.

So instead I said, "Maybe she is sorry for us. But that doesn't change what she said about not being able to know whether it used to be as good. When we get as old as she is, I bet we'll be telling everyone how great the old days were and forgetting how lousy they are."

"Do you think so?" he asked me. But he was a lot more cheerful.

"Sure," I said. "That's what always happens when you get old. You look back and think how wonderful it used to be."

"I couldn't stand it if I thought I didn't have a chance," Vinnie said, and I knew I'd been right about not talking to him straight. I'd never met a kid like Vinnie, I mean a kid who thought about everything before he did it. It was what they call weak, in a way.

I don't mean I don't like Vinnie, because I do. I like him better than any kid I ever met, I guess. But I know he's not as strong as a lot of dumb kids I know. In Palm Beach, kids only think about what they want the next minute, but they're tough. Vinnie has a lot of other ideas, but there's plenty he can't face.

I guess that was why Mrs. Appleton talked to him the way she did. And maybe that was what she was telling me when she looked at me the way she did. Anyhow, I hope I got the message the way it was supposed to come.

So we walked along the road, and Vinnie was thinking about what Mrs. Appleton had said and I was thinking about her. I guess that's the difference between kids like Vinnie and kids like me. One kind thinks about what people say and ideas, and the other thinks about what people are underneath. But I figure it's what people are that makes them say what they say, so it's like looking at the motor instead of the outside of the boat. I don't mean I thought about Mrs. Appleton like she was a motor. She was an old lady who knew what she was doing. But it was the knowing that got me and it was the doing — what she said — that got Vinnie.

"I'd like to grow up and do something," Vinnie said after a while. "I don't want to live the way my mother and father do. I want to work. And if you work, you have to have a goal. You have to have a goal even if you're playing tennis — like winning — and what I'm talking about is more than that. But it's like tennis in another way, because you have to think it's worth something, the way people think tennis is worth playing. If nothing's any good then your goal is no good. That's why I have to figure it out now."

"I don't see what you're all upset about," I said. "Sure, there's trouble around, but like Mrs. Appleton says, there's always trouble. You have to just . . . go ahead."

I sounded like Mr. Stokely, but that was what Vinnie needed. He was all cheered up, and started telling me how he wanted to be an engineer or something when he grew up, and I was wondering whether what I had said to him could be true. I mean, if it made him feel better, maybe it was right. But I didn't know how to try it on myself.

CHAPTER FOUR

VINNIE'S MOTHER was reading a magazine out on the patio when we got back and he introduced me to her. I don't think she knew who I was. I mean, I don't think she connected me with Dad, because there were no jokes about cows and all that.

But the cow thing started when they all got together again. They can do the nights and days on their own, but they need a sort of outside topic to get rolling about five or six o'clock when they all get together on the patio and start putting down the first cocktails.

It was just like at the Waverlys', and they started talking about me and seeing my first cow and someone said that Mexico was full of cows and someone else said, "Why not a safari to Acapulco?" And Mrs. Ming was yelling about *vacas*, which is Mexican for cows.

It was too late to get off that night, but they made the reservations for the next day and everyone went to bed early. That happens sometimes. When Dad is going hunting or something in the glades, or sailing down to the Keys, he will go to bed sometimes at seven or eight at night so he can get up at five in the morning. And then his picture's in the papers and he's called the "noted sportsman," and he looks pretty good in those pictures because he's always got a tan, and he's had a long sleep the night before, and you'd never know he was up as late every night as he usually is.

Vinnie and I were up later than they were. We watched television until about midnight, and then rang for the maid and she brought us ham sandwiches and milk. She was a different one. I never saw service like that in a house. Usually you have to go to a hotel to get service like that.

Well, of course, I could hardly wake up in the morning. About seven, there was Dad hanging over the bed, shaking me and laughing a mean laugh and saying, "You lie around all day and then you can't get up in the morning."

And I said, "Yeah, just like Achilles, and he didn't turn out too bad."

"Achilles who?" Dad asked me. He's never heard of anyone who lived before 1950 or something.

He always gets me one down like that. He stays up late and drinks, and after about two weeks of it he plays a round of golf and has a good night's sleep and there he is at seven in the morning looking like Tarzan. And I take care of myself and never drink and get up every morning at six, except maybe once a month when I've stayed up late watching TV, and that's the one morning in the month *he* gets up before I do.

But he's doing what they call burning the candle at both ends. I'm sure of that, and before you know it he'll have a heart attack or something pretty close to it. You read about them all the time.

We took rented helicopters to San Francisco and caught the jet for Acapulco there. There were about twenty people in the party, and one kid. Me. They were all in sports coats and blazers and the ladies had on Lillys and they had fishing rods and tennis rackets and all that stuff, and they looked as though they never took a drink, and I was only a kid and I looked awful. I was in the same shorts I'd been wearing since I left Palm Beach, and I had the same shirt on, too, and the same tennis shoes. They were old and I had no socks on.

I'd meant to borrow some clean clothes from Vinnie, but there hadn't been any time. I'd meant to tell him goodbye, too, but there wasn't even time for that. He would have been sore, though, getting waked up at seven in the morning after staying up late, and I couldn't blame him for that. So I was just as glad I didn't wake him up.

Anyhow, they were all laughing at me, even

Clive, because I looked so lousy, and Dad said, "I pretend I don't know him."

And I thought to myself, well, it wasn't my idea to come on this trip.

When we got on the plane, they practically took it over and I sat next to a lady who wasn't in the party. Usually I sat next to Clive, but not this time. The lady next to me was quiet and old and a little like Mrs. Hollins. Except that she really wasn't. She wasn't smart, I mean. She was the kind that pretends to like kids, but doesn't get it. Like she was reading the paper and she said to me, "Don't you just love *Peanuts* and Charlie Brown?"

"I think it's a fake," I said. "Always the same thing. The dog who thinks he's someone else. And the rest of them."

"Oh, but they do stand for something else," she said. "They're *symbols*."

And then she went on about how it all meant something else, and I finally said, "So what? I mean, why do things have to stand for something else? Why can't they be straight? Like, *Peanuts* isn't for kids, it's for grown-ups. Mrs. Hollins says if you want to find out what's going on today, read Art Buchwald. And she's right. All the kids I know read Art Buchwald and none of them read *Peaunts*. It's like *Pogo*. It's

for grown-ups and poor people, like a dream,
but Art Buchwald is for real."

And then she got sort of upset and started
asking me who I thought I was to look down my
nose at Charlie Brown. I told her I was a
neglected kid. It was the first thing that came
into my head.

"Neglected?" she said. "Well, you do look
rather unkempt, but I'm sure you're not neglected."

She was about fifty years old and had on a
suit and wore glasses and I could tell she didn't
know about places like Palm Beach at all.

"Sure I'm neglected," I said. "I can tell I am
because I've got so much Crazy Foam."

"Crazy Foam?" she said. "What's that?"

"It's something to make you want to take a
bath," I said. "They put it in a toy, like a mon-
key with big fat lips or a rooster, and you
squeeze it and Crazy Foam comes out. It looks
like shaving cream and it's a detergent, I guess,
but it's got no smell or feel. Anyhow, you're
supposed to get in the bathtub with it, but it
never works that way. You just sit around and
squirt it at some other kid. But only neglected
kids have it." I was thinking that a girl like
Natalie Gregg *wouldn't* have Crazy Foam
around.

"Well, I don't see why Crazy Foam means

you're neglected," she said. "I just don't understand that at all."

"Well, it does," I said. "Just like Super Stuff. I guess you don't know what that is, either."

"No," she said, "but I'd like to."

"It's a powder that makes a jelly when you get it cold, and it comes out bright pink. Then you warm it up and drop it in another kid's mouth while he's on the floor, and it feels good when it falls on your stomach, too. It's just something to do when you don't have anything else to do with your hands. It only costs about a dollar and it can ruin about a thousand dollars' worth of furniture. Because it gets all over everything and sticks. So why would any parent buy it for a kid unless they wanted the furniture ruined? But you know they don't want their furniture ruined, so you know they're not thinking when they give it to you. And if they're not thinking, they're neglecting. See what I mean?"

"No," she said. "I think you're ungrateful and don't appreciate your advantages."

I was about to say, "You call Crazy Foam and Super Stuff an advantage?" But I didn't, because I could see by then that she was too dumb to get anything. That's another thing that always gets me. You know people with money are dumb, and so you think the others might not

be, but they always are. Dumber, if anything.
Except a few, like Mrs. Hollins. But she must
have had money once herself. Otherwise, she
wouldn't know all she does about kids like me
and their parents.

Then Dad came back to the seat to chew me
out about my clothes, and the lady started to say
something to him, and he cut her off in that way
he has for people who don't have money, and
she sort of puffed up.

"You didn't give me time to get any other
clothes on before we left," I said.

"Well, you could have bought something in
the last three days," he said. "All you've been
doing in lying around watching TV."

"I haven't seen a store since we left," I said.
"And besides, what would I use for money?"

"You're always after me for money," he said.
"I wish you had more sense of responsibility."

What could I say to that? Nothing, so I kept
my mouth shut and he finally told me he'd take
me to get some clothes as soon as we landed in
Acapulco.

"When are we going home?" I asked him.

"When I get good and ready!" he yelled in a
loud voice. "Don't push me!"

When he was gone, the lady didn't say anything to me for the rest of the trip.

CHAPTER FIVE

I CAN'T SEE why people think Acapulco is so great. It's noisy and all cramped up together and the television is lousy. But Dad and his friends really go for it. They say it's "so simple, like Palm Beach used to be." Most of the party stayed in the same hotel but some of them slopped over into another place. As soon as we got there, they all grabbed their fishing rods and tennis rackets and went off to exercise. Dad forgot all about getting me new clothes, of course, so I just sat around in what I had and watched Mexican television. And like I said, it's not much to watch.

After a while I gave up and went out by the pool. All the people had on bathing suits and they were just as tan as the people in Palm Beach. All except me, and I was just as white and flabby as I am in Palm Beach. But there was nothing else to do, so I found a place in the shade and just sat there.

Some old man came along and sat next to me and asked me if I didn't have any bathing trunks, and I told him no. He said he could get me a pair, but I said I didn't want any. He had a funny accent, not Mexican but foreign. He asked me what I was doing in Acapulco, and I told him I was there to see some cows. I had a hard time explaining what it was all about, but it was kind of fun because he was pretty smart and seemed to get what was going on. At least he laughed in the right places and all that.

Then he told me he had a ranch outside Mexico City where he raised bulls for bullfights and I was welcome to visit it if I wanted to learn anything about bulls and so on. I thanked him and told him I was pretty well tied to Dad and had to go where he went. So we talked like that for a while and then he went off.

There were some American kids around the pool and we all started talking together, but they weren't rich and there wasn't much I could say to them. You can tell they aren't rich when they think everything is so great and they're doing everything for the first time. This one kid about my own age, Carl something-or-other, kept telling me about some new house his father had built in a place called Beverly Hills and I thought it was a castle or something from the fuss he made about it. But then I could tell it was that kind of house where everyone has his own bedroom and there are only two left over for guests. When people really have money, there are extra rooms all over the place. They need the extra rooms for parties. You can't give a big party without plenty of extra rooms.

I didn't tell Carl that, of course. If kids don't know anything, you can't tell them. I learned that a long time ago.

So I kept my mouth shut and went off to "take a walk around the ward," like Mr. O'Connor says. He's a friend of Dad's and he always says that when he leaves the house. "I think I'll take a walk around the ward."

There wasn't much to see and I got sort of tired, so I sat down on a bench in a kind of little park to watch the people walking by. After a while a couple of American hippies sat down next to me and started talking to each other in whispers. The boy was about twenty-one and had a beard and long hair and a yellow shirt and earrings and corduroy pants, and the girl was about the same and had long hair and jeans and neither of them had any shoes on.

I couldn't help but hear what they were talking about even if they were saying it in whispers. They were flat broke and didn't have enough money to buy anything to eat and didn't know how they were going to get back to America and on and on. It was kind of sad, because you could see they were really scared.

Finally I couldn't stand it anymore, so I butted in.

"Listen," I said, "there are lots of ways you can get money."

They looked at me with those wide eyes hippies have, and said, "How, like?"

"Beg," I said. "These Mexicans go for beggars."

It was true — that's about all you see down there.

"We tried that," they said, and then they introduced themselves.

"My names is Hermes," the girl said.

"And I'm Ganymede," he said.

They looked at me like they were waiting for me to tell them who I was, and they had those funny little smiles that hippies have. Like they know so much more than you do. I could tell the names they had said weren't their real names. They sounded like something out of the Greek heroes book that Mrs. Hollins reads to us from, and I thought, well, if you want to be Greeks I'll be one, too.

"Glad to meet you," I said. "I'm Achilles."

It's the only Greek name I know, but it's one of the best known. Everyone recognizes it. The hippies did, and kind of nodded and looked at each other and said "Beautiful!" while they shook hands with me. I had stuck out my hand and said, "Glad to meet you," like a poor person, and so they sort of had to shake it. I don't know why I did that, except that I thought if they want to pretend with me I'll pretend with

them. I mean I'm from Palm Beach and my
family is rich, and hippies are really just workers. But they want to act like they're not workers, like they're rich but just fooling around.
They're really pretending they aren't poor but
rich, that's what I think the hippies are all
about. Anyhow, if people pretend to be rich I
figure I might as well pretend I'm poor, and talk
like a farmer. It kind of balances the whole
thing up.

"What are you doing here?" Hermes asked
me.

"Gee, I don't know that myself," I said. "My
dad came down to Mexico to work in an oil
field and then he lost his leg in some industrial
accident and now he's in a hospital here and I
have to work to support him."

"What do you work at?" Hermes said.

I couldn't think of anything, so I said, "I
train dogs."

So we were talking like that and they were
asking me how much money there was in dog
training and I said there was lots if you got the
right dogs, and then an American in a white
suit walked by and Ganymede jumped up and
ran over to him and held out his hand and said,
"Would you help a fellow American who's down
on his luck a little, like?"

And the American in the white suit just kept walking. He didn't even stop.

When Ganymede came back, he said, "You see, I try to beg, but it doesn't work."

I couldn't get over it. "You mean you beg like that?" I asked him.

"Sure," he said.

"You'll never get anything that way," I said. "Don't you know Americans like that don't think you're a fellow American? They think you're un-American. They don't want to have anything to do with you."

"But that's not right!" Hermes said.

"Who cares whether it's right?" I said. "That's what they think, and if you're asking them for money that's what you have to work off."

"But what else can I say?" Ganymede asked in kind of a whine.

"You have to say something that fits," I said.

"Like what?" Ganymede said.

"Gee, I don't know," I said. "Say you're a great artist or something."

So the next American that came by got that. Ganymede hopped over to him and said he was an artist and needed money to buy paint and all that. He didn't get anything, but the man talked to him for a while before he went. I told Ganymede that showed he was on the right track, but he said a miss was as good as a mile.

We were still sitting there when the first American came back, the one in the white suit, and he had a Mexican cop with him and he was jabbering in Spanish to the cop and then the cop started talking to Ganymede in slow English and telling him he was begging without a license or something, and because he was bothering people he had to come along to the jail.

Then Hermes flew at the cop, and the next thing you know another couple of cops showed up and grabbed her. I was trying to look like I was just watching, but the man in the white suit pointed at me and they grabbed me, too. So all three of us went to jail and were pushed along in front of a judge in a little room, and the cops talked to him and the man in the white suit talked to him, too, all in Spanish. Then the judge said something to another pair of cops and they took us out of that room and down some long halls and then into the part of the jail where they had the cells, and locked us in one. All together.

There were Mexicans in the cells all around us and they were talking Spanish. I couldn't understand a word. Ganymede was pretty upset and Hermes was, too, but they were trying not to show it. I didn't say anything because I thought I knew what was coming, and sure enough, in a couple of minutes they quit trying not to show how upset they were and started in on me. Especially Hermes. She yelled at me for telling Ganymede to beg, but she didn't call him Ganymede anymore. She called him Jim.

I tried not to think about anything. I knew Dad would get me out sooner or later, but I was more afraid of him than I was of the Mexicans. So I just sat there and kept my mouth shut, and let Hermes keep shouting.

After about an hour, the two cops came back and opened up the door on our cell, and Jim and Hermes started out, but the cops pushed them back and pointed at me. So I walked out, and the cops locked the door again, and Jim and Hermes were screaming like maniacs behind us while we walked down the hall.

The man in the white suit was outside and he told me the Mexicans had decided I was too young to hold, so they were letting me go. But I should watch my step, he said, and all that.

I could have walked right out, but there was something so big-shot about him that it made me sore. And I was sort of upset about what Hermes had said about my getting Jim to beg. I didn't care that much about Jim or her, but I knew there was some truth in what she said. I *had* had something to do with it.

So instead of walking away, I said to him, "Well, you've sure made a big mistake."

That's the way Dad talks to people when he's after them, and I hoped it would work for me.

"What do you mean?" he said.

"You don't think a hard worker like Jim would be begging unless he had a good reason, do you?" I asked him.

"He's not a hard worker," he said. "He's just a hippie."

"That's what you think," I said. "He's not a hippie. He's only *pretending* to be a hippie."

"Pretending to be a hippie?" he said, like he hadn't heard me right.

"Sure," I said. "He thinks it's the only way he can dress if he's going to be able to make any money."

"But why doesn't he work?" he said.

"Because he has to stay here until his dad gets out of the hospital," I said. Then I told him that Jim's dad had had his leg cut off out in the oil fields, and the hospital bills were so terrific, and Jim was really what they call a clean-cut kid, but he'd had to give up a good job in America to come down here and watch after his dad and he couldn't work here so he had to beg and that was why he and Hermes, his wife, were dressed as hippies. I got so worked up telling him about it that I began to believe it myself.

"So look at him now," I said. "Locked up in this lousy jail. Dressed like a hippie with his hair down to the middle of his back. Two months ago he was a clean-cut young American with a good job. Selling insurance. Now look at him. A hippie! All because he wanted to help his dad. And you've given him the final turn of the knife. You've finished him, mister!"

"I see," he said, kind of pulling on his lower lip. "I see." He stood there thinking for a minute and then he said, "Let's go across the street."

So we left the jail and went across the street to a little restaurant and I had some kind of sticky drink with no alcohol in it and he had a regular drink.

"What did you say your name was?" he asked me.

"Uh, Frank," I said.

"You any relation to those two?" he asked me.

"Naw," I said. "But our parents are friends."

"Well, Frank," he said, "I'm Harley Burleson, from El Paso, and I'm glad you told me all this. I wouldn't like to think I was causing a worthy young man a lot of trouble on top of what he already has."

When he said that he seemed pretty decent, and I was ready to tell him to forget it, that Jim and Hermes were just hippies after all. But then I remembered that he had had me put in that jail, too, and it wasn't his idea to let me out. I was out because of my age, not because he had done anything. And when they did let me go, he'd given me a lot of big-shot talk. So I decided he didn't deserve anything, and that there was something I had to settle with him. Not because of Jim and Hermes, but because of me.

"No," I said, "you wouldn't want to do that. And besides, it wouldn't look so good."

"What do you mean?" he said.

"Well," I said, "those things get around. People find out that Mr. Burleson, from El Paso, has put a clean kid like Jim in jail and it doesn't look so good."

"No," he said, and started thinking again. I knew then he was hooked. Like Dad says — they live in the pocketbook. Those people with just a little, maybe a couple of hundred thousand, they care much more about it than anyone with money does.

"I'll drop the complaint," he said. "I'll have them turned loose."

I didn't say anything, and he kept looking at me.

"Well?" he said.

"I don't know," I said. "Jim is pretty quiet,

but Hermes is wild. I don't want to scare you, mister, but she might make Jim sue you for false arrest, or whatever they call it."

"They can't do that!" he said, but his face was red and I knew he thought they could.

"You couldn't have known about Jim's dad and all the rest," I said, "but that doesn't mean people might not hold it against you. You know, people who'd say, 'Who does he think he is, having American kids arrested in Mexico for begging? Why isn't he in El Paso tending to business instead of running around causing trouble down in Mexico?' "

Well, he huffed and he puffed, but in the end he asked me if I thought Jim would take a little "contribution" to his dad's hospital bills.

"I think that would be a nice idea," I said.

"About two hundred and fifty?" he said.

"I'd go a little higher," I said.

"Three hundred?" he said.

"I'd say five to be safe," I said.

So he got up and said he was going back to the jail and would I come, too. I said no, I had to get home, and he said goodbye and went back across the street to the jail. I went around to the rear of the restaurant and waited there in a place where I could see the front of the jail but no one could see me.

In about fifteen minutes they all came out

together. Mr. Burleson, Jim and Hermes. Jim and Hermes were looking kind of confused and Mr. Burleson was rattling along about how expensive hospitals were and how he'd do anything to help. You could tell he was ready to go past five hundred. You'd think Jim and Hermes would have been playing right up to him, but no, they had those dumb looks on that hippies can get, and they were just staring at him like a couple of squares.

There I had *shown* them how to beg, and they were too dumb to get it. I had handed Mr. Burleson to them, but instead of grabbing his five hundred and looking for more, they were trying to find a way to put it back in his pocket. If I had been them, I would have been thinking how great it would be to team up with me and do *that* kind of begging all over Mexico. Get put in jail by Americans and then have me go to work for the money. But hippies never think like that. I guess you'd say they have no business sense.

I waited until they were out of sight and then I started back to the hotel. I didn't really care what happened to Mr. Burleson or Jim and Hermes, when I thought it over. I'd settled up with Mr. Burleson for putting me in jail, and in a way I'd settled with Jim and Hermes, too, and that was all there was to it.

When I got back to the hotel, the American kids were still around the pool. I didn't want to talk to them, so I went in the bar and had two dishes of ice cream. It was not bad ice cream.

Dad came back about five o'clock and was in a pretty good mood.

"I think we'll head back tomorrow," he said. "Remember that you've got school on Monday."

"I know it," I said.

"I realize you haven't seen any cows on this trip," he said, "but that was only an excuse, anyhow. I wanted to take a trip with you, just the two of us, so we could get to know each other. There's no way to do that in Palm Beach because there's so much pressure and running around. But this is different and I hope we can do it more often."

I really thought he'd flipped. But I was wrong. He was serious. He's like an actor that way. One minute he's from Palm Beach, and the next he's like one of those fathers whose kid's in Little League, and then he's the father whose kid's got a problem. You never know what's coming.

He kept on talking, but there was a Mexican band playing pretty loud and most of what he said from then on was drowned out, and I sort of tuned out myself.

Then he went up to change and I lay down

for a while on a bench behind a wall in the
lobby. About seven he and the rest of the party
got together in the cocktail lounge and I could
tell they were going to have a big night, so I
borrowed all the comic books I could from Carl,
and went up to my room and ordered dinner up
there. I had a steak and it was only fair. Then
I read the comic books for a couple of hours
and went to sleep.

CHAPTER SIX

IT WAS SUNDAY the next morning and when I woke up I decided to tell Dad we *had* to get back. But I knew he'd be sleeping late, so I'd have to wait until he got up. I went down to the pool and there was no one there except Mrs. Ming. She was sound asleep in a chair with her mouth open, and I could tell she hadn't made it all the way to bed after the party.

Then she started snoring and a couple of the Mexican waiters started laughing, and I thought I better do something. I didn't know her very well, but she's Vinnie's mother and I think he'd do the same for my mother. So I told the waiters to carry her up to her room. At first they didn't want to, but I was pretty firm and they finally said O.K. They didn't know how to pick up the feet and the head, so I had to show them. I could have carried one end myself, because I usually carry Dad's feet when Charles and I find him on the lawn when we're leaving for school, so I know how. But I thought it was a better idea to make both Mexicans do it so there wouldn't be one of them standing around with nothing to do but laugh. It was a mistake. I should have taken the feet, as it turned out, but how was I to know that?

Anyhow, the Mexicans picked her up and started to carry her and then she woke up and started screaming "Let me go!" and they panicked and teetered around and then the three of them went into the pool with a whopping splash.

She came up yelling and half the people in the hotel were yelling "Shut up!" from their rooms and it was worse because it was Sunday morning.

I didn't know what to do, but I went over to the pool and tried to help Mrs. Ming out. She was still yelling and I tried to explain to her what had happened and then she turned on me.

"How dare you tell those men to pick me up!" she hollered, loud enough to hear her in California, and the guests started yelling all over again.

She was so wet she couldn't work on me too long, though, so she finally marched upstairs. The Mexican waiters were sore at me, too. They got out of the pool after she left, with their hair all plastered down and their uniforms pretty soggy.

It wasn't a very good beginning to the day, and so I sat around and cried. I was still moaning and sobbing along to myself when Dad came down in his robe. I thought he was going to be sore, but he was in a pretty good mood. He always fools you that way.

"Helen Ming looks great," he said. "You really fixed her up."

"I tried to help her," I said. "It was those dumb Mexican waiters. They dropped her."

He laughed. "I told her that. I know you were only trying to help. But what a help!" He laughed again. " 'That stupid kid of yours!' she yelled at me, and I said, 'Are you telling *me?*' "

"She was down here snoring like a busted rocket, Dad," I said, "and all the waiters were laughing at her."

"Let's forget it," Dad said. "I'm up now, so I might as well have a swim."

He had his trunks on under his robe, so he hopped in and splashed around for a while.

Then Clive came down and sat next to me. She didn't look so good, and I wondered how she keeps her job in the movies. She doesn't have any money at all, so she has to work. She's a starlet. And they all call her "The Starlet" and make fun of her, so she's about on my level. But she's old enough to take off, so I don't see why she hangs around.

Then the old man with the bull ranch who had talked to me the day before came along, and he started talking to me again, and Dad got out of the pool and joined in. When he found

out the old man had a bull ranch he got excited
and told the old man he'd give anything to see
the ranch because he was so crazy about bullfighting and all that. I could tell the old man
wasn't too excited about having Dad visit the
ranch, but there wasn't much he could do about
it because he'd already asked me, so he finally
said that would be fine.

He thought Dad meant in a couple of weeks
or something, and when Dad told him it had to
be today he said it was impossible. But Dad said
he'd hire a plane and the old man could come
with us, and then the plane would fly him back
after we went into Mexico City to catch a plane
for Miami. Dad can get you so involved in those
plans that you don't know whether you're coming or going and the old man just couldn't hold
out all morning, so he finally gave in and said
O.K.

He wouldn't have said O.K., though, if he'd
known it meant the whole gang, but by the time
he knew that, it was too late to back out. They
were all down in the lobby in an hour, most of
them in a lousy mood with big hangovers, but
ready to go. I've noticed it before. Rich people
are always ready for anything new. Especially
if it costs money, like renting a plane, and
means going some place they haven't been. And
they all love bullfights, of course.

Even Mrs. Ming was there, cleaned up and dried off, and telling everyone about bullfights. I had to hand it to Dad. He really has a way of getting people to do what he wants when he feels like it. If he hadn't always had money, he might have been able to have a pretty big job.

We couldn't all get into one of the planes they had for rent, so we had to take two. The old man who owned the bulls, whose name was something like Sanchez, was in our plane and everyone was asking him questions about raising bulls and he was trying to explain, but they were all drinking by that time and no one was listening to the answers. After a while, they didn't even ask him any more questions. He just sat there, looking at them and then out the window and then at me. He didn't look very happy and I was kind of sorry I was the one who had been the cause of it in a way.

Then Clive was sick and there was a big mess cleaning it up and Dad yelled at her and the plane smelled awful the rest of the way. Mr. Sanchez just looked at the floor.

We landed at a little airfield near his ranch and there were three big old American cars there to take us over to the ranch place itself, what they call the hacienda in Mexico.

It was pretty nice. Nothing special, but nice and simple. A lot of leather chairs and bulls'

horns around. His wife and his two daughters
were there and they were upset at the gang he
was bringing home, you could tell, but they
were calm about it. If they were going to chew
him out, they were going to do it later, I
thought. But they didn't look as though they
did much chewing.

Well, then we went out to see the bulls. The
big ones were out in a field and too far away
to see close, but there were some young ones in
a pen near the barns and they let them into a
little round corral and Dad peeled off his coat
and jumped down in and he was trying to use
his coat the way a bullfighter uses his cape and
the young bulls were chasing it and Dad was
grunting at them and everyone else was squealing and yelling. Mr. Waverly kept yelling *Olé!*
and Mrs. Ming would yell it right back at him.
Mr. Ming wasn't there, so I guess he stayed in
Acapulco. Mr. Sanchez looked more upset than
ever, and the men who worked for him were
smiling as though they didn't know what to
make of it. Then one of those young bulls came
tearing into Dad with his head and knocked him
flat, and a couple of Mr. Sanchez's man dragged
him out of the ring and he looked plenty green.

He hadn't been stuck with a horn or anything, just butted with the head.

"I'm all right," he said. "It happens to the best of them."

"You looked great in there, Barry," some guy said.

"I used to be pretty fair," Dad said. "Getting too old, now."

Everyone said that wasn't true, and they all started telling him how great he had looked and all that stuff.

It was about four o'clock in the afternoon then, and I was really hungry and so was everyone else, but Mr. Sanchez wasn't feeding anyone. He really wanted us to go, and finally everyone knew it, even Mrs. Ming.

So we all said goodbye, and Mr. Sanchez had a tight little smile while he shook hands. When he said goodbye to me, he just rubbed the top of my head and shook his own head, the way you do when something is true but you can hardly believe it.

I wanted to tell him I was sorry, but I couldn't with all those people there. I couldn't, anyhow, to tell the truth, because I never say what I mean. Unless it's like a joke. It's a habit I have.

But I think he knew I was sorry. Because of the way he looked at me and shook his head.

Then we were in those big old cars again and heading for Mexico City. Everyone was starving, but every place we passed on the road looked so lousy that no one wanted to stop. We got some beer and cold enchiladas and guzzled them, but it only made us hungrier.

By the time I got to the airport I was wild. I couldn't sit still and I was crying all the time and everyone in the car with me was just about crazy. Dad wouldn't ride with me. He got in another car, and some guy in the car I was in said, "Your father showed real courage out there today, so why can't you control yourself?"

I was so wild I said the first thing that came into my head. "That wasn't courage," I said. "He just doesn't know any better."

Lucky for me, this guy was so dumb himself that he couldn't figure out what I'd said.

When we got to the airport I was so weak that I could hardly drag myself to the restaurant. I was afraid that Dad would be so sore at me for crying that he'd cut me off with a pork chop or something. But I was lucky again. He went into the bar with most of them, and I was able to order for myself in the restaurant. I ordered *two* filets and two baked potatoes, one with butter and the other one with the chives, and knocked all that off and then had a malted milk and a piece of apple pie. And drank about a gallon of ice-cold milk. It wasn't cold enough when they brought it, but I got them to bring a bucket of ice cubes and kept throwing them in.

It took me about two hours to get back to normal.

They were all drinking in the airport bar and I went outside on the cement where they keep the planes and was hanging around there when I heard a noise behind me and there were about fifty Mexicans running as fast as they could and behind them was the biggest bull you ever saw. He had his head down and his horns were coming along like two whopping ice picks, not more than a foot off the cement and sharp like needles at the ends. His feet were making the worst noise on that cement I ever heard. It sounded like about six football teams chugging out of a locker room. But they only go out to play, and he was something else.

It looked so crazy to see a bull like that in the middle of all those airplanes and everything, and the first thing I thought was, "It can't be happening." But it was. I found out later that he was being shipped somewhere and he'd busted out of his cage and started off. Now he had his eye on one little Mexican who couldn't keep up with the others, and he was following him like a rocket hunting for heat. The little Mexican was twisting and turning and going this way and that way, but the bull was right behind him and gaining about ten yards every second.

I was over to one side and the bull was just going by. He didn't see me and I was near enough a plane so I figured I could duck behind a wheel anyhow, and I thought to myself, "Maybe I can do something to pull him off that Mexican and then get back to the wheel." I ran sideways out from where I was and waved my arms and yelled something — I can't even remember what it was. Then I was jumping up and down and feeling all that fat around my middle jouncing around and all that steak and milk slurping around inside me, and wondering if I'd ever be able to get my feet off the ground again. But finally the bull saw me and he swerved around like a Cadillac in a chase in the movies and came zooming right at me. I started back to my airplane wheel, just like I planned, and then I could see that I'd made a mistake and I wasn't going to get to the wheel before the bull got to me. I could hear those feet pounding behind me and that wheezy snorting that bulls make and I thought I'd had it. At the last minute I jumped to the left and he went by me at about three hundred miles an hour and I could smell his skin and all the rest of him, dry and like iron, and the noise was awful.

It gave me time to get to the wheel, though,

and I got around on the other side of it just as
he came back. He'd overshot by about fifty
yards and when he turned he'd slipped and gone
down and slid on that cement for another fifty,
but he was so fast that he was up and on his
way back about the same time I got behind the
wheel.

He wasn't stopping for anything. When he
got to the wheel he sank one of those horns
about three feet into that big airplane tire and
there was the biggest Whooooooshhhhhhh you
ever heard. He tried to pull his horn back out,
but he'd gotten it hooked up inside the tire so
he couldn't pull it loose. So he was stuck, and
the air was pouring out on both of us, and the
main part of the plane was coming down and I
thought I was going to be squashed underneath.

But it could only go down so far and then it
stopped and there was still plenty of room. My
face was plastered up against the other side of
the tire and I could hear the bull snorting and
wheezing and then I could hear some other
snorts and wheezes and it was me. I was making
about as much noise as he was, and my heart
was pounding like a jackhammer and all that
steak and stuff was still swirling around inside
me like the tide going out the Palm Beach Inlet.
The bull and the ox, what a pair, I was thinking

to myself in that crazy way things come to you when you're all excited like that.

He twisted and turned and pushed and pulled, but he couldn't get that horn out. Part of the trouble was that cement, because his feet kept slipping. And anyhow, it was such a crazy thing that had happened to him, so he didn't have any experience in how to handle it.

When I was pretty sure he was stuck for keeps, I slid out from behind the wheel and started for the airport building. I didn't stop until I got behind a wire fence, and then when I turned around I saw some of the Mexicans creeping out from where they'd gotten to, because they'd figured out he was stuck, too. Some of them came over to me and they were talking about it in an excited way, but I couldn't understand what they were saying. They kept wanting to shake hands, and I did that a couple of times. But I got away as soon as I could, because I knew that if Dad found out I'd had anything to do with a bull after the trouble he'd had, he'd skin me alive.

So I went up on the observation deck and watched them work on the bull from there. I was so shot I could barely stand up, but it was pretty interesting, so I kept watching. They brought his cage around and patched it up with chains, and then they roped him from the rear

and hauled the rope with a tractor and finally
the horn came out. They had so many ropes on
him by that time that there was nothing he
could do, and they got him back into the cage
without any more trouble.

Dad and the rest of them came out of the
airport to watch it, and they were right down
below me. The guy who had gotten sore at me in
the car looked up and saw me and said, "You
can come down here if you want — there's no
danger."

Dad looked up then, too, and shook his head,
like I was too much, but I didn't say anything.
There was nothing I *could* say, if you came
right down to it.

CHAPTER SEVEN

IT WAS MIDNIGHT or something when we finally took off, and no one was "feeling any pain," like Clive said. She talks like that.

She was sitting next to me, and she told me she was so worried about Dad and all that. About the bullfight and running around so much.

"I don't see what you're so worried about," I said. "No matter what Dad does, he never gets killed."

"I think he'd be happier if he had a job," she said.

"I don't think so," I said. Sometimes I wondered the same thing myself, but I wasn't going to tell her so. Instead I explained to her how no one ever worked in Palm Beach.

"Everyone would think Dad was crazy if he worked," I said.

"But where does their money come from?" she asked me, kind of confused.

"They *inherit* it," I told her. "About twenty years ago or something, the grandfathers made money, like mine did, and they left it in estates, so now none of the fathers in Palm Beach have to work."

She kept asking me questions and I told her

how everybody knows *where* their money comes from, like Tommy Alterdale's from the Alterdale Container Corporation, somewhere in Wisconsin, and Natalie Gregg's from Gregg Shipping Lines, in New York. But Mr. Alterdale never goes to Wisconsin, and Mr. Gregg never goes to the docks or anything when he goes to New York. She just couldn't get over it and I could tell she'd never thought much about money.

We were supposed to change in Houston, but there weren't any more flights that night, so we had to go to a motel. And that was where the real trouble started.

I had a room to myself and I was sleeping along fine, but about eight o'clock in the morning there was a big noise at the door and it opened and about sixteen cops came flying into the room. One of them grabbed me and said, "Barry Olmstead, I arrest you in the name of . . ." and all that stuff. I was kind of half under the covers and my hair is sort of long, so I guess he thought I was a man.

"Aw, can it!" I said. "I'm a kid."

"Where's this Barry Olmstead?" this cop said, looking at me hard.

"I don't know," I said, and started to cry. "That's my dad."

Then another cop poked his head in and said,

"He's in a room on the other side," and they all ran out and pounded across the courtyard.

I got up and got dressed as fast as I could. Dad did some pretty silly things, but he was careful to steer clear of crime. So I couldn't figure out what he'd done.

When I went over to his room, there were about a hundred people in it. Cops and some of the party and the people from the motel. And about a thousand outside, standing and staring.

The cops let me in but Dad was getting dressed in the bathroom, so I had to wait like everyone else until he came out. The cops were all grinning at each other, but I didn't see what was so funny. Neither did Clive, because she was shivering around and biting her lip and her eyes were red.

When Dad came out he was grinning too, though, like the cops. But he was sore underneath, I could tell. Not at me, but at some ex-wife or his named Fernanda who lives in Houston.

"Now, Franklin, I want you to listen carefully," he said to me right in front of all those people, like Gregory Peck in some old movie on television talking to his son before he goes out to chase some crooks. I thought Dad was doing it to make an impression, and I knew he was when he put his hands on my shoulders and

looked into my eyes like he was going to tell me
I had leukemia or something.

"Your Dad has been married before," he said,
real slow, like I didn't know he'd been married
about six times, "and my former wife heard
from some friend of hers in Mexico that I was
coming through Houston, so she is having me
arrested on a charge of not paying her alimony.
Which is absurd. She doesn't have a leg to stand
on, and I'll call Charlie Kipper and he'll ar-
range bail and we'll be flying out this afternoon. No sweat. The only problem is whether
you have enough comic books to last from now
until then."

All those people were listening to him, and
admiring the way he was so cool and everything, and when he put that in about the comic
books they all broke up and started laughing
and smacking each other on their backs. Even
the cops.

Dad handed me a twenty-dollar bill then, and
he was looking so noble even if it was faked that
he made me feel I was George Washington's kid
or something. He got me talking the same way,
too. I was looking right back in the eye at him,
and I said, "You can count on me, Dad. I'll stay
here until you get out. Whether it's one hour or
one day or one month."

That speech *really* made a hit. They were all

saying "That kid's got guts" and "You can depend on that kid" and excited things like that. They almost cheered.

I should have left it right there, but I got sort of carried away and said, "Shall I call Mom?" and Dad looked at me hard and the crowd started muttering around.

Then Dad went off with the cops and I was left at the motel. The rest of the party cleared out about noon. Some of the ladies kissed me goodbye, and a couple of the men shook hands, but most of them just left. The party was over, and they were all thinking how they were going to explain it to their wives or husbands or someone. I know, because Dad and Mom are always explaining to each other like that.

Clive was walking out like she didn't know I was still there, but I yelled at her and she stopped on the walk. Then she kissed me and blubbered and said, "You poor kid."

And I said, "What are you talking about, Clive? I'm a rich kid."

That made her blubber some more and it was about five minutes before she got in her taxi. She was squeezing me all that time. She's about the most nervous poor person I know, I guess.

Then I went back to the motel pool, and there were a whole bunch of poor people there, but I sat around anyhow because there was no place

else to go. I didn't feel like starting with television until later.

One of the poor girls had a colored doll, and
I remembered some kid in Palm Beach telling
me that poor kids really go for colored dolls.
Rich girls don't. They like expensive dolls in
carriages and things like that.

The poor girl's name was Mary or something,
and she got tired of the colored doll and started
asking her mother for a new doll.

"I got you a new doll yesterday," the mother
said. "Stop bothering me."

"It's broke," this Mary said.

"How can it be broke?" the mother said.
"I only got it for you yesterday."

"I can't help it," Mary said. "It just broke."
Then she started to cry.

They do that in poor families. The parents
are sort of helpless or something and never turn
the kids off the way they do in rich families.
The girls get up in the morning in poor families
and howl around and about ten o'clock their
mothers drive them to get a new doll. You can
see them like that in Burdine's in West Palm
Beach every morning. I guess it's what keeps
business going.

I got tired of being at that pool after listening to all that yelling about dolls for a couple
of hours, so I decided to get something to eat.

I would have liked to eat at the pool, but those
kids were too much. When you travel in America, you never see kids except at motel pools,
but then you don't see anything else, even early
in the morning.

There was a drugstore across the highway
and I went in and had a couple of grilled cheese
sandwiches and a malt. I was just finishing up
when a really nutty-looking bunch of people
came wandering in. Right in the middle was a
little guy, about forty, in a raincoat that looked
like a tent and was made of different colors,
and hanging on his arm was a skinny woman
with long hair and big sunglasses and a kind
of wild grin and a coat that looked like it was
made of old alligators. There were about fifty
people jumping around those two, listening to
them and laughing at everything they said. The
little guy was talking to them in kind of a funny
way, with his voice all tightened up, and the
woman with him kept that wild grin wide open,
like she couldn't turn it off if she wanted to.

The whole bunch crowded into all the booths
in the place and were asking for drinks like
champagne with their hamburgers, the kind of
stuff you can never find in a drugstore unless
it's in Paris. And this one was in Texas! They
knew they couldn't get those drinks, you could
tell by the way they smiled little smiles at each

other when they asked for them. They just wanted to bother the waitresses, who were all Southerners, the kind who don't know when other people are kidding or not. They kept saying, "No, we don't have any of that," in that patient way they have, with straight faces, that finally calms nutty people down.

Then a man with his stomach showing between his shirt and his pants came running in and shouted, "Here he comes! Here comes Baxter!" A bunch of them jumped up from where they were sitting and headed for the door. And just as they got there it opened and a kid about my age walked in. They all started crowding around him and telling him how great he was, and he was smiling kind of a silly smile and scratching his shoe on the ground, and that just drove them wild and they told him he was just too much, and he grinned and wiggled his foot some more and they couldn't get enough of it. I knew I knew that kid, but I couldn't place him for a minute. And then it hit me right between the eyes. It was Dale Tifton!

I opened my mouth to call out to him, but then I closed it right back up again, because there was something I didn't get. It was Dale, all right, but he wasn't being like himself. He was acting so sort of shy and *nice*, and Dale isn't nice at all. And the clothes weren't right.

Dale is always dirty, but it's dirt rubbed into expensive clothes. Now he was a lot cleaner than he is in Palm Beach, but the clothes looked cheap.

So I didn't say anything and just sat there, and in a little while he looked over and saw me. He didn't show any sign that he knew me at all. I guess he has that kind of control and never shows any surprise at anything because he's seen so much. And has been in so many spots where he would have been in real danger if he'd showed his feelings. He's really trained, like a hood on TV. He just looked at me for a second, and then he looked back to the gang around him and talked with them for a while, and then he went over and sat down with the little guy with the raincoat that looked like a rainbow and the woman in the alligator coat.

I didn't move. I thought he'd figure out some way to say something to me if he could, and he did, with the smoothest trick I ever saw. Especially if you knew what was going on, like I did a little later. First he started pointing at me, and the little guy and the woman looked at me, and then he talked to them, with his face all screwed up like some kid on TV asking for another guinea pig in his bedroom.

And they talked to him and then they all looked at me again and talked some more, and finally some other guy, who'd been hanging over the back of their booth listening to it all, started over to say something to me, but Dale stood up then and I could tell that what he was saying was that *he'd* come over.

I was noticing all that, but I wasn't looking right at them. I was sort of turned around half-way in my seat at the counter, fooling with what was left of the potato chips and the pickle on my plate and watching what was going on out of the corner of my eye. So when Dale showed up at my table, I was able to look surprised.

"Say, uh," he said, "could I, uh, talk to you for a minute?"

"Sure," I said, and I didn't say any more, because about ten of the rest of them were hanging around listening.

"Well, uh," he said, "we were wondering if you'd uh, like to help us out a little this afternoon. We, uh," and then he stopped, like one of those kids on TV programs who keep stuttering around trying to tell their father that their dog is caught in a bear trap and it's starting to snow and all that. It was Dale standing there in front of me, all right, but he was talking like a kid who's never had anything.

"Go ahead," I said. "I'm listening."

"We're making a movie here," he said, "and we wondered if you'd play it in."

"Why?" I said. "Because I'm so fat?"

"No," he said. He was sounding a little more like Dale now. "They say you've got an interesting face — it would look good on the film. You could come with us this afternoon and take a look and see what you think."

"Well, that sounds pretty interesting," I said. It was all I could do to keep a straight face now. "But I have to be back here by five."

"Oh, you will," he said.

So he went back to tell them the good news, and after they ate we went out to where they were shooting. Dale and I went in the same car with the little guy and the woman, and so we still couldn't talk. The little guy kept jabbering away to Dale and calling him Baxter and telling him how wonderful he was.

"When I think of my own boyhood," the little guy said, "and then I look at Baxter. Well, I just can't believe it! I just can't believe I was ever that . . . *innocent*." Then he laughed and sneezed and got red in the face and even his laugh was all tightened up, and his little legs were waving in the air.

The woman asked me what my name was, and I said it was Frank, and she said, "Frank what?" and I said, "Frank Alterdorf." I used

Tommy Alterdorf's last name because I figured that if there was going to be any trouble it might as well be tied to a kid I didn't like at all.

"What does your father do, Frank?" she asked me, smiling at me like I was a new boy friend. She was older than my own mother and she was smiling at me and gushing all over the place like a teenager.

"He's a pro football player," I said. I don't know why I said it except that I felt so big and fat and dirty in the car that a pro football player for a father was about the only way of explaining me.

"Oh, how interesting," she said.

"You going to play pro football when you grow up?" Dale asked me. He was leaning forward where they couldn't see his face and he looked just like the real Dale. Deadpan, but with the hardness in his eyes.

"Aw, I don't know," I said. "All those bumps and bruises. Dad wants me to keep up the family tradition, but I might do something else instead. I might even go into raising cows."

"Boy, that sounds like fun," Dale said. "Sitting there on a farm of your own and milking cows every night."

There was something about the way he said it that almost broke me up again. I had to talk

about something else, so I asked him what
this movie was all about. And he told me.

It was some story. The little guy's name was
Jiminy Crockett, and he's a famous personality
in the country. I've seen him myself on TV and
it just shows you that you can see people on
TV and never know them in real life when you
meet them. Anyhow, Jiminy — and that's his
real name, Jiminy — was born in Texas and
was a kid there before he went to New York
and got famous. So some movie producer said,
"Let's show the whole world where Jiminy
Crockett came from, and what kind of life kids
used to have in the old days down in Texas."
And all that.

So they're making the movie in Texas and
*Dale Tifton is playing the part of Jiminy as a
kid!* I almost passed out when he got to that
part.

"He's *me!*" Jiminy was screaming in my ear.
"I don't mean he's me the way I was, because I
was always different in my own way, but he's
the *me* I would have been if I had stayed in
Texas and played around with the tumbling
tumbleweed." He talks like that.

"You were never like Baxter," the woman
said.

"Yes, I was," Jiminy said. "You didn't know
me then, so you can't judge."

"I know you now," she said. Her real name is Garrett Mirabell and she's a famous personality, too. I've never seen her on TV, but she's been there.

"I guess you were pretty lucky to find Baxter to do the part," I said to Jiminy. I was hoping he'd tell me how they'd connected up with Dale, but he didn't.

"Baxter is a wonderful boy," he said. "He's me and not me, all at one and the same time." Then he laughed and squirmed and Garrett looked out the window.

When we piled out where they were making the movie I finally got Dale off to one side.

"You're a long way from home," I said.

"So are you," he said.

"I suppose so," I said, "but I'm on my way back."

"I'm not," Dale said. "I got so fed up that I just hitchhiked out a week ago. I was thumbing through Tallahassee and this Jiminy Crockett and a couple of his friends picked me up. They were driving to Houston because the kid who was supposed to play the part drowned in a lake and they had to find another one fast. I hadn't been in the car ten minutes before they offered me the job."

"What about parents?" I asked him. "Don't they have laws about it?"

"I told them I'd run away from an orphanage," he said. "They won't turn me in because they're against everything like that. They'd rather see a kid starve than put him in an orphanage."

"I didn't mean them so much," I said. "I meant the people who run the schools and the rest."

"They don't pay any attention to you if you're in the entertainment world," he said. "Besides, they don't care about anything like that in Texas."

Well, I couldn't get over it, and I told him so. Dale Tifton in the movies, it was like me in Congress. I asked him what he'd do when the movie came out and everyone in Palm Beach would be seeing it, and then they'd know where to look for him.

"I'll have my own money then," he said, "and they won't be able to do anything."

"They must be looking for you all over the country," I said.

"But they're not going to find me," he said, "and you're not going to tell them."

"No, I won't say a word," I said.

"You better not," he said.

That's what's wrong with Dale, when you come right down to it. You tell him you won't do something and instead of believing you, he has to make a threat. That's what I mean when I say he's been out on the streets too long.

"You've sure turned into a good actor," I said, sort of to change the subject.

"It's easy," he said. "And they're all so dumb."

He's hard, Dale is, and he has no respect for people. I don't have much myself, but I can *imagine* what it would be like to respect people. Dale can't. He can't think of people being any other way than the way they are about all the time. I guess that's the difference between me and Dale.

Then I told him about Dad being arrested and everything, and he just grunted.

"You've got it easy, though," he said, "compared to that old man of mine."

"I don't know," I said.

"Well," he said, "if you want to break out, I could get you into this movie."

"I thought you were kidding about that," I said.

"In the beginning I was, because I wanted to talk to you," he said. "But they went for it. They thought you were as beat-up as a kid can get, and they like that. Garrett liked the way you look from the side, too. 'Don't miss that profile,' she kept saying, 'so aristocratic under all the fat.'"

"Looks aren't everything," I said. "But they can't just stick me in anywhere."

"They do what they call 'write you in,' " Dale said. "They invent a part for you and slip it right in."

I'd never known that, and then Dale told me a lot of other stuff about how the movie business works. He knows all about it. They can write you out, too, when they get tired of you or when they're having a fight with each other. They write people in and out all the time.

Then Dale had to go to work. They were making a scene with him as Jiminy Crockett when Jiminy comes home from digging up worms or something one morning, and he starts to talk to this old cowboy who's supposed to be so wise and smart. It wasn't a real cowboy, of course, but an actor. He was a good friend of Jiminy's, too, and they all treated him with respect. His name was Jefferson Black. I'd never heard of him, but they all acted as though he was something big.

So they got the cameras all ready, and then Dale came along the road and Jefferson was sitting out in front of his shack and they waved to each other and then Dale came right up to the shack and he and Jefferson Black talked about how hot it was and what a beautiful day it was going to be and a lot of stuff like that. Jefferson

Black was good. Before they started the scene
he was talking about books and art with a regular accent, and now he was talking like a Texan
and moving around like an old cowboy. He was
good, but Dale was something else. I've seen a
lot of TV but I never saw an actor like Dale. He
was looking at Jefferson Black and talking to
him like he'd been a poor kid for about fifteen
generations. No one who didn't know who he
was could have guessed in a million years that
he was Carl Tifton's son and that his uncle runs
American Cynadine and that his great-grandmother was Holly Tifton and that the family has
had millions of millions. Not millions, but millions *of millions*. You just couldn't have guessed
it. No one could have. Least of all Jiminy
himself.

At one place, Jefferson Black said something
like, "A boy can learn a lot from horses," and
Dale didn't say anything for a while, making
you wonder what he *was* going to say to that,
and then he said, "More'n a horse can learn
from boys, I reckon." Real slow, in a perfect
Texas accent and with a look on his face you
couldn't believe!

I was standing behind where Jiminy Crockett
was sitting, and he was snuffling and blowing
his nose and wiping his eyes and thinking he
was seeing himself out there. And I looked

around and the whole crew was pulling long
faces and half of them had tears in their eyes.
Even Garrett was crying. It was the wildest
thing you ever saw.

When the scene was over they *clapped*. They
all stood up and clapped, and Dale pretended
he thought they were clapping for Jefferson
Black and sort of waved his hand over at him,
and Jefferson Black swallowed that all the way
and acted like it was just the cutest thing he
ever saw. And then he came over to Dale and
pointed to *him* and then to the people who were
clapping and Dale turned around like he was
saying, "Who, *me?*" and he did it so perfectly
that they clapped all the more. I think Dale's
got a real future in that acting.

When Dale and I got together in his dressing
room in the trailer a little later, I told him that,
only instead of saying, "You have a great
future, Dale," I said, "You have a great future,
Baxter." I said it that way as a joke, but you
just can't joke with Dale. He looked at me as
though he was going to sock me and then he
said, "Don't call me Baxter except in public."

"How'd you pick that name?" I asked him.

"None of your business," he said.

"All right," I said, and I thought that would
end it, but it didn't. He had to come over and

grab me by the shirt and say, "And don't forget
it."

"Aw, cut it out," I said.

He thought that meant I was scared, so he
jabbed his finger into my stomach, and said,
"I'll cut it out when I'm ready and not before."

If there's one thing I can't stand it's a finger
jabbing me like that in the stomach, and without thinking I gave him a shove. I'm fat, but
I'm awful strong, too, and he sailed across the
trailer and banged into the other side.

"You'll cut it out *now*," I said.

He came tearing back and lit into me, but
I got my arms around him and began to squeeze.
That's where I have my strength, in my arms,
and in a little while his face began to get red
and I could feel his legs getting wobbly.

"Had enough?" I said.

He shook his head up and down to say he had
and I let him go. He kind of sagged down into
a chair and just then the door flew open.

It was one of the directors or whatever they
call them. "You all right, Baxter?" he said to
Dale. "We heard some noise in here." He looked
at me in a tough way, but I just grinned at him.

Dale could barely talk, but he passed it off
like nothing you ever saw. "I was practicing a
scene," he said. "Frank was helping me."

The ordinary kid would have broken down

and put the finger on me. Especially when they
all thought he was so hot, and he could have gotten them to do anything to anyone. But not
Dale. I guess that's what they call breeding.
I've never seen a kid to equal him there. Not
even Natalie Gregg. She has background and
she's well-bred, and that seems as far as you
can go, but then Dale comes along and makes
you wonder if there isn't even more to it. Like
once his grandmother or someone was as well-
bred as Natalie, but the Tiftons couldn't get any
better bred so they started back down. But even
when they hit bottom again, like Dale, they
have more breeding than when they were on
top, like Natalie is now. It's like you have to
lose it to really have it.

Well, to get back to what was going on, the
director got out of the trailer, even though he
was still a little suspicious. Dale and I didn't
have much more to say to each other and he had
to get back to work, so I said I'd go back to the
motel. He asked them to drive me back.

"Well, Frank," said Jiminy, "how about it?
Would you like to join our happy little company?"

"Gee, I don't think I can, Mr. Crockett," I
said. "I just remembered I've gotta do something with my dad for the next few days."

"Play football with him?" Jiminy asked me,

and I couldn't make any sense out of that at
all.

But Dale remembered I'd said my dad was a
pro football player. "He's got to make a road
trip with his dad," he said. "The team is playing in Miami." He said it so naturally you had
to believe it. Dale can do stuff like that like no
kid you ever saw.

When we said goodbye, we were both acting.
He's really good, of course, but I was doing my
best and it wasn't bad. The whole crew was
watching us so we had to do something. And it
made a good private joke for the two of us.

"So long, Frank," Dale said. "I hope your
dad makes a lot of tackles up there in Cleve-
land."

"Thanks, Baxter," I said. "And I hope you
keep on acting just the way you've been acting
today."

It was just the way grown-up poor people
talk to each other, but no one noticed that, of
course. I thought it was pretty good what I said
about Dale acting, because he was acting about
twice as much as they thought he was. But what
he said about "your dad" making tackles was
what they call genius. The idea of my dad working that hard was so funny that I almost broke
up for about the fifteenth time. If I'd stayed
there anymore I would have, so it was good
I didn't take the job.

CHAPTER EIGHT

THE DRIVER let me off at the motel and Dad still wasn't back. I wasn't worried about him, because he hadn't done anything he couldn't get out of by paying up his alimony. Or making bail. I was going to take a nap, but they told me at the desk that there were two guys from the Houston television station waiting to see me. They wanted to do an interview with me because of Dad being arrested that morning. I really didn't care that much about the nap, so I said O.K. They had a portable camera and a few hot lights and we sat there in my room and I talked with them. They asked me a lot of crazy questions and I gave them answers that were just as crazy.

Like they said, "How big is your home in Palm Beach?" And I said, "About a hundred and thirty rooms and my mom doesn't like too many servants so she cleans them all every day herself."

Then they asked me about Dad being a sportsman, and I told them he was one of the best bear hunters in the world. "He goes up to Alaska to shoot those bears that are really big, and he can knock them off with one shot because he knows where to shoot. Most of the guys who hunt those bears take about ten shots, but Dad found out that was a waste of time if you know where to put just one good slug. In what they call the Achilles' heel, because that's where Achilles got it when he stopped crying and came out of his tent to fight. I don't mean it was in the bear's heel, because the Achilles' heel is only a way of saying where the weakest part is. In the bear, it's the *knee*. The Achilles' heel is the *knee*."

"The *knee?*" this guy says, leaning forward like he hadn't heard it right.

"The knee," I said. "These bears have got some kind of artery there, and if you hit it just right all their blood rushes out in about two seconds and they're dead. I guess that's a secret that's worth about ten million to bear hunters, but I'm pretty sure Dad would want them to know it because there's no way he can make that kind of money out of it and he doesn't need it anyhow. The only thing about shooting them in the knee is that you have to be able to stand the sight of blood, because there sure is a lot. Sometimes Dad comes home solid red from top to bottom, and Mom looks up from her cleaning and says, 'That must have been a big one, Barry,' and Dad says, 'I don't know if I can take it much longer. The look on those bears' faces. And the way they die. . . .'"

"So your mother and father are happy together?" this guy asks, kind of interrupting me about the bears.

"Well, sure they are," I said. "People are always happy when they get what they want, aren't they? Mom has her house and her cleaning and her cooking — she's always bending into the oven to look at her pies and cakes and the rest — and Dad has his bears and his blood, so why shouldn't they be happy?"

"How do you feel about your father being in jail?" he said.

"How would any kid feel about it?" I said, and started crying.

Then he gave me a handkerchief and I blew into that for a while and then he asked me how many kids "of my class" live in Palm Beach.

"We don't eat off gold plates or anything like that," I said. "So I don't want you to get the wrong idea. But I guess we do have it pretty soft, a lot easier than kids do anywhere else. I know a kid who's got a television set in the ceiling of his own bedroom, and another kid who can go to Europe any time he wants because he's got his own credit card. But some of the kids are restless. They get their values all mixed up. Some of them would even rather be poor."

Then he asked me if I knew anything about poor kids.

"I sure do," I said. "I spend a lot of time thinking about poor kids and what they do and everything."

"Would you tell me what you think a 'poor kid' is? Can you define what you mean by 'poor kid'?"

"A poor kid," I said, "Is a kid that likes sewing machines that don't work."

"I don't quite follow you," he said.

"Even when there's money to buy real ones," I said. "Like when a poor mother has one of those machines that does all the stitches and her daughter says 'I love to sew,' but she doesn't want to sew on the real one. She wants to *pretend* to sew on a plastic toy sewing machine. Poor people always want to pretend. I guess that's what I mean."

"It's an interesting example," he said.

"I didn't make it up," I said. "I saw it happen just like that at a dentist's house in Palm Beach."

"But surely a dentist who lives in Palm Beach is not a poor man," he said, just like Clive did when I told her.

"This one was," I said, and I told him all about the house and the watermelon seeds and the crossword puzzle on the wet table.

"I see," he said, but he didn't seem too happy about it.

Then he asked me some more about Palm Beach and how people lived there and I let my imagination take over.

Right in the middle of it Dad came in and blew right up, of course. He yelled at the television guys and said they had to leave, and that he'd keep the interview they had with me from being shown on the air if he had to buy the whole state of Texas to do it, and all that kind of stuff.

After they were gone, he chewed me out for about three hours and I cried right straight through.

"What did you think you were doing?" he kept asking me.

"I thought I was helping you," I said.

I wished he'd wallop me and get it over with, but he was still sort of noble from the morning and wanted to keep talking.

He was out on bail, just like he said he'd be, and we were supposed to fly out that night.

"Unless I have to stay here to keep your face from appearing in just about the most public place I can think of," he said.

"I guess you mean a television screen," I said.

"I wonder how much of the dirt will show,"

he said in about as nasty a way as he could.
He was right there, though, because I was really
a mess. Rachel would have to work for about
a week to clean me up, I could see that.

Well, he made a lot of telephone calls and
yelled about "invasion of privacy" and finally
said he thought he had it under control.

"I guess they'll play ball," he said, "but you
never know with those reporters."

We had dinner together. I guess it was one of
the few times Dad and I ever ate together. We
had it in the motel room because Dad was
afraid there'd be more reporters if he tried to
go out anyplace. He had his steak medium-rare
and I had mine rare. It was only fair, even if
we were supposed to be in Texas and all that
beef.

Dad slipped over to his room after dinner to
pack up, and he was right, there were reporters
hiding around in the bushes outside and they
tried to talk to him. But he just kept going.

They followed our taxi to the airport and
trailed us all over the place before we got on the
plane. We didn't say anything, but they got
plenty of pictures. I could see that was bothering Dad because I was looking so lousy. I would
have taken a shower and tried to clean up, but
what was the point when I had to get back into

the same clothes again? So I just stayed dirty and let it go at that.

"Well, that's over," Dad said when we got on the plane. We were sitting together and that made him nervous, I guess. It was about the only time we ever did sit together because usually there are other people in the party and he sits with them.

So he had nothing to do except start in on me again, and he did.

"I try to help you with a school project," he said. "I go to a lot of time and trouble — and spend a lot of money, too, incidentally — and what thanks do I get? Very little. None, to be honest. Then I get arrested and my son goes on television to talk about my private life. . . ."

"I didn't talk about your private life," I said. "I don't know anything about it."

". . . to talk about something, then. Just what did you talk about?"

"Oh, I told them what a good hunter you are, and stuff like that. Nothing personal."

"I'll bet. Anyhow, there's my son on television and I'm in jail all day. For what? Because I tried to help him with his homework."

"Aw, gee, Dad!"

"And I'll bet you haven't even done it."

"I haven't had time."

"Haven't had *time!*" he yelled and turned

on me like I was some sort of Hitler. "You've
had a *week*. And all you've done is lie around
in motels looking at television. Or talking to
television reporters."

"Well, what can I write about?" I said. "I
never did see a cow, you know."

"You never saw a cow!"

"No."

We argued about that for a while, and then
he admitted I was right, that I hadn't seen one
of those cows that makes butter even if I might
have seen a lot of the other kind, the ones
that the steaks come from. If he hadn't admitted
I was right, I was thinking of saying I hadn't
been able to find any paper, but I was pretty
sure that would have caused more trouble so
I don't think I would have. Anyhow, I didn't
need to.

Then he had a couple of drinks and cheered
up a little, and told me some long story about
when he was playing polo at Gulfstream when
he was a kid and falling off his horse and how
it made a man of him. I couldn't follow it. Then
he went to sleep.

I stayed awake for a while and then I went to
sleep, too. It had been a long day, about the
longest since we left, so I was pretty pooped and
I guess that's why I started dreaming about
going back to school and standing there while

everyone was handing in their compositions on the cows and the milk and the butter.

"Well, Franklin," Mrs. Hollins said, "I hesitate to ask."

"You'd be wasting your time," I agreed with her.

"Franklin," she said, "what *were* you doing the past week?"

"I went to Mexico with my Dad," I said.

"What for?"

"Ah . . . bullfighting," I said, like it was the first thing that came into my head.

"You went to Mexico to the bullfights?" she asked me, like she couldn't believe any kid, even me, would be so lazy.

"Dad made me go with him," I said.

"Didn't you tell him you would be missing school days?"

"Sure, but . . . well, he said he thought it would be more of an education . . . you know, like seeing things happen the way they do in real life . . . instead of reading about it in books."

"I see. Perhaps he's right. The important question, I suppose, is whether you learned anything from the trip."

"Oh, I did," I said. "I learned a lot."

"There's only one way to find out," she said, and I could see what was coming, even in the dream with all that swirling around. "Why don't you tell the class about the bullfights? Start at the beginning, from the time you sat down in your seat and the music started."

"Well, ah . . ." I said, and was pretty well stuck. And hot all over, because I didn't know any more about bullfights than I did about cows and butter. Some voice kept telling me I had told the lie about seeing bullfights to get out of the composition about the cows, and now I was in another jam. Mrs. Hollins's face was big in front of me and I knew she knew all about it, as usual. She wasn't saying, "Isn't Franklin fortunate to be able to go to Mexico just like that to see the bullfights." That was the way the other teachers talked, because they were all jealous of rich people and can't stand the way we can do what we want and when we want.

So I was standing there with my mouth open and the other teachers were filling up the room and yelling about how lucky I was to be able to go to Mexico when I wanted, and Mrs. Hollins said, "If you don't want to tell us about it, Franklin, then write a composition about the bullfights."

She was smiling at me and the other teachers were fading out, and then the whole trip was going past me in a hurry — the helicopter at the

Waverlys', and Ed with his gun and the Indians, and Clive being sick, and Vinnie Ming, and Mrs. Appleton, and Acapulco and the hippies and the man in the white suit from El Paso, and Dad with his bull and me with mine, and the cops in Houston with Dad and the whole party laughing, and Dale Tifton and Jiminy Crockett and the movie — and Mrs. Hollins's face smiling behind it all. So I was smiling back, even if I did feel lousy, because I knew Mrs. Hollins didn't expect anything from me like a composition, because she knew there was nothing inside me. I knew I was a permanent washout then, and I don't think any kid likes to find that out about himself. I know I didn't. The voice was telling me that as lousy as things get, though, you're never at the end if you're a kid. Then the voice stopped and it was like it was written in gold letters on a wall, saying that everything can get one degree worse for a kid. Especially if you're rich, and a socialite. It was all there in gold letters marching right across the wall: EVERYTHING CAN ALWAYS GET ONE DEGREE WORSE FOR A KID, ESPECIALLY IF THAT KID IS *YOU*, OX OLMSTEAD, BOY SOCIALITE. And Mrs. Hollins was smiling and I was feeling lousy and all the kids and teachers were there again and they were all howling. It was a scene.

CHAPTER NINE

WE GOT to Miami about midnight and rented a car to drive up to Palm Beach. It was a pretty good night. I mean, it was clear and all that, and it had that soft smell that Florida has. We had a convertible, so you couldn't miss the smell.

It only takes about an hour to drive up, so we were there pretty soon. Sooner than Dad wanted to, I could tell, because he kept looking up at the stars like they were the last ones he was going to see for a long time.

There was a big party going on at the house when we got there. We could hear the orchestra playing about a mile away and there were about a hundred people dancing out on the patio. There were so many cars that we couldn't even get into the driveway, so we had to park our car in the street where most of the cars were. One of the cops who was on duty came over and said, "This is a private party." Then he recognized Dad and was kind of embarrassed. But it wasn't his fault. The cops in Palm Beach know you by your car, and when they see a car they don't know, they figure they don't know the person in it. And we were both kind of worn out and not looking too normal.

We went into the house and there weren't
many people there because most of them were
outside on the patio. But there were enough so
that we got some pretty curious looks. "Hi,
Barry," they said to Dad, but you could see they
were wondering why he was coming into his
own house looking like he didn't belong there.
And what I was doing tagging along like I
didn't know who I was.

Then Mom stepped in from the patio, and I
thought that was going to be it, but she just
said, "I've been looking for you two. Been to the
Keys? Why don't you change and join the party,
Barry."

"I guess I will," Dad mumbled.

"You look good, Franklin," she said to me,
and that got a big laugh. I was thinking she
didn't know the difference between "good" and
"well," and trying to remember myself what it
was supposed to be. So I went to bed. I don't
know what Dad did.

The next morning it was the same old grind.
I got up and felt just as lousy as I always do. I
had only had about two hours' sleep, and I was
shot, but I couldn't sleep any more so I got up.
The sun was shining the way it always does,
and I went downstairs to watch television like I
always do, and the house looked like a couple
of armies from Cuba had been camping there.

It doesn't *always* look that way, but it always looks that way after there's been a party.

Then Rachel called me for breakfast, the way she always does, and she took one look at me and then she grabbed me and took me upstairs and threw me in the bathtub and worked on me for about two hours and it did feel pretty good to get clean again.

"I don't see how you can stand being so dirty," she said. "Weren't you someplace where you could take a shower? Don't tell me you couldn't take a shower in a *week*?"

"We were roughing it," I said, and it was a lie in a way because we weren't in a camp or anything, but in another way it wasn't a lie.

"Where were you, anyhow?" she asked me. "Mexico," I said.

"I guess it's pretty dirty down there," she said.

"Did you wonder where we were?" I asked her.

"I told your mom you weren't here, and she said I must not be looking in the right places, but after a couple of days she said you must have gone to the Keys or someplace like that, so I wasn't exactly worried. How come she didn't know you'd gone to Mexico?"

"I don't know," I said. "I guess Dad didn't tell her."

"Well," she said, "I guess you're as clean as you can get. Now you get dressed and I'll give you breakfast and you can go to school."

"I'll be late," I said. "It's nine o'clock already."

"Better be late than hang around here all day," she said.

I was going to argue and then I remembered that Mom and Dad would probably both want to chew me out, so I said O.K.

Breakfast wasn't very good, any more than it ever is. Mom makes Rachel buy some kind of cheap pork sausage at Publix and feed it to me and the servants. Everyone else in the house gets what they want for breakfast, but I have to eat the kind of cheap sausage that shrivels up. The eggs were all dried up, too. I had been thinking that we were having lousy food when we were traveling around, especially down in Mexico, but I'd forgotten how lousy a cook Rachel really is.

Charles came in the kitchen and was lounging around and looking me over and making a lot of dirty cracks about kids in general, and how they are so weak today.

"I don't know about that," I said. "I bet that when you were a kid you couldn't spend all your time jetting around and eating lousy food and not getting enough sleep and being in the same clothes all the time. You don't know how tough a kid has to be today."

That sort of shut him up and then we went out and got in the car and were all ready to start for school when I turned around and saw Mom sound asleep on the back seat. We didn't say a word to each other, because we both know what to do. Charles got out and opened the back door and got his hands under her arms and pulled her head out and just as her feet got to the door I grabbed them and we carried her right in and upstairs and dropped her on the bed.

Then we went back downstairs without a word and got in the car, and I was thinking that if those Mexicans could see how it looked when it was done right they might have learned something. But they probably wouldn't have because if people can't figure out how to carry a drunk on their own, how can you teach them? It's got to be one of the simplest things in the world to figure out, and you're pretty dumb if you can't do it.

When we drove down the driveway we were both looking out of the corners of our eyes at the piece of lawn where Dad usually is if he doesn't make it, but he wasn't there. We never have had to carry both of them the same day,

but I know Charles wants to. It's like winning
a bet with himself or something.

"What am I supposed to do with the car your
father drove up from Miami?" he asked me in
a typical way. Nasty, I mean.

"Ask him," I said.

"I thought you might know," he said. "Didn't
you drive up with him?"

"Naw," I said. "I walked."

Then he got sore. I could tell, even though he
didn't say anything. He wanted me to cry because I'd had to carry my own Mom up to bed
at ten o'clock in the morning. But I wasn't
going to give him that pleasure. I only cry when
it bothers people. When I know that someone
likes to see me cry, like Charles, I don't.

So I got out at school without a word, like
always, and he didn't say anything either, so it
was just like every morning.

A couple of kids I know asked me where I'd
been and I said, "Mexico." Just that. "Mexico."
I didn't see any point in going into it any more
than that.

I went into the class and everyone was there,
and Mrs. Hollins said, "Why, Franklin, how
nice to have you back. We were beginning to
worry about you."

And I could tell she knew everything that had
happened, so I burst into tears and bellowed so

loud that even Natalie Gregg looked worried and Tommy Alterdale forgot to yell "Rowboat!"

Then I went out on the balcony, as usual, and Mr. Stokely came by underneath, as usual, and asked me what I was doing. I said I was watering the plant exhibit and off he went. Nothing ever changes.

ABOUT THE AUTHOR

JOHN NEY has been a professional writer for more than twenty years, working on novels, nonfiction and movie scripts. He lives in Austria with his wife and three children. He is fond of gardening, fishing, swimming and cycling.

Mr. Ney brings a very cosmopolitan background to *OX*. He was born in St. Paul, Minnesota, and brought up in New York and St. Louis. For a time he lived in the Blue Ridge section of Virginia. In 1949 he moved to Italy, where he worked in the young motion picture industry. He later lived in England, Spain, Switzerland and other European countries, as well as in Jamaica in the West Indies and Palm Beach, where Ox begins his journey.

was that he'd remar...
I was notich...
ight at them, I...
way in my se...